# WHAT YOU DESERVE

## ANYTHING FOR LOVE - BOOK 3

## ADELE CLEE

Copyright © 2016 Adele Clee
All rights reserved.
ISBN-13: 978-0-9935291-5-3

*What You Promised* (excerpt)
Copyright © 2016 Adele Clee
All rights reserved.

Cover designed by **Jay Aheer**

**Books by Adele Clee**

To Save a Sinner

A Curse of the Heart

What Every Lord Wants

The Secret To Your Surrender

A Simple Case of Seduction

**Anything for Love Series**

What You Desire

What You Propose

What You Deserve

What You Promised

**The Brotherhood Series**

Lost to the Night

Slave to the Night

Abandoned to the Night

Lured to the Night

**Lost Ladies of London**

The Mysterious Miss Flint

The Deceptive Lady Darby

The Scandalous Lady Sandford

The Daring Miss Darcy

**Avenging Lords**

At Last the Rogue Returns

# CHAPTER 1

$\mathcal{T}$ristan Wells, seventh Viscount Morford, stood alone in the drawing room of Lord Mottlesborough's town-house, watching the musicians unpack their instruments in preparation for the concert.

Lady Mottlesborough came scuttling into the room, her hand flying to her chest when she discovered him loitering behind the door. "Good heavens, my lord. You gave me a fright. What on earth are you doing hiding back there?"

Tristan blinked rapidly. Judging by the sight of the excessively large turban wrapped around the matron's head, he should be the one clutching his chest. Beneath the voluminous folds of exotic silk, he imagined she was as bald as the day she was born.

"I am taking a moment to gather my thoughts." Under present circumstances, she could hardly question his motives. Whilst mourning the loss of one's brother rarely affected a gentleman's social calendar, a more subdued countenance was only to be expected.

The lady gave a rueful smile. "I assume your mother has pestered you to leave the house again this evening." She gestured to the musicians and whispered, "I doubt praise for their skill has dragged you here. They are hardly the talk of the Season."

He snorted. "As you are aware, my mother makes no secret of the fact she is keen for me to find a bride."

With Tristan being the only male member of the family, his mother's eagerness for him to produce an heir bordered on desperation.

"I have heard she has a particular lady in mind."

"She has many ladies in mind," Tristan said with a derisive chuckle, "as long as they're from good breeding stock." In truth, he was beginning to feel like a reluctant bull being herded into a field full of heifers.

"I understand your mother's urgency to see you wed," Lady Mottlesborough said. "Despite her mourning period, no one would cast aspersions on the decision to protect one's heritage. Indeed, we are all aware that one's duty and responsibility must come before everything else."

Tristan knew better than anyone the sacrifices one must make for the sake of patrimony. But with his mother still in full mourning, it prevented her from attending functions, and as such, he found it more preferable to wander the corridors of other people's houses than to remain in his own. He also came in the hope of finding more stimulating conversation, something that did not involve talk of flounces and other such fripperies.

"For the moment, I have been granted a reprieve," he said with a weary sigh.

Lady Mottlesborough nodded. "And so you linger in the shadows in the hope the ladies won't find you." She raised a curious brow. "Or perhaps it is one particular lady you wish to avoid. Where is the lovely Miss Smythe this evening?"

Miss Priscilla Smythe *was* lovely. She possessed a sweet, kind disposition, a generous heart and a pretty countenance. Whenever he thought of kissing her, his mind conjured images of summer meadows, birds chirping merrily and chocolate macaroons. On the whole, he imagined the experience would be pleasant, if not particularly memorable.

"I believe you will find her surrounded by a host of other ladies just as eager to discuss the merits of ribbon over lace."

Lady Mottlesborough nodded despite the hint of contempt in his tone. "I am afraid we ladies tend to take the topic of haberdashery extremely seriously." She chuckled. "Sewing and embroidery are subjects dear to my heart."

Tristan wondered if that was why she wore the turban. Perhaps she carried her frame and threads around with her in case she found the evening's entertainment too dull. "I'm certain that when you stumble upon Miss Smythe, she will be only too happy to hear all about it."

The matron's suspicious gaze drifted over his face. "Perhaps your interest lies elsewhere. Perhaps you have another lady in mind."

Tristan knew to have a care. Friendly overtures were often used to drag snippets of gossip from unsuspecting fools. Many unwilling parties had been forced into an arrangement simply to stop loose tongues from wagging.

"This evening, I am only interested in listening to a soothing melody whilst enjoying my freedom for a little while longer."

He wanted to say that he had no interest in titles or land. He had no interest in the begetting of an heir, or to be the husband of a woman who failed to ignite even the smallest spark of passion in his chest.

Lady Mottlesborough winced at the sound of the harsh chords as the musicians warmed up their bows. "I hate to be the one to ruin an evening, but the Baxendale Quartet are quite mediocre when it comes to Haydn."

"Then I thank you for the warning," he said with a smirk, "and shall take care to sit near the back."

"A splendid idea. Had I not been the hostess, I most certainly would have joined you." Lady Mottlesborough's attention drifted to the door. "And now it seems your plan to go unnoticed has been foiled, my lord."

Tristan followed her gaze to see Miss Priscilla Smythe and her companion, Miss Hamilton, enter the drawing room.

Lady Mottlesborough tapped his arm with her closed fan. "I'm afraid there is no escaping now," she said before turning to greet the other guests pouring in through the door.

He suppressed a groan as both ladies smiled sweetly and came over to join him.

"I simply knew we would find you in here, eager to secure the best seat." Miss Smythe chuckled sweetly, her golden ringlets bobbing up and down in response. She turned to Miss Hamilton. "Lady Morford said he simply adores Haydn."

"You all know me only too well," he said, his affable tone bringing on a bout of nausea. In reality, none of them knew him at all.

Tristan sighed inwardly. It had not taken him long to fall back into the feigned modes of conduct he despised. Showing enthusiasm when he had none came easier to him than he thought.

"I wanted to introduce you to Mr. Fellows," Miss Smythe said, fluttering her lashes, which appeared to be a nervous habit as opposed to a means of flirtation.

"Mr. Fellows?" He made an attempt to look interested.

"My friend's brother. Do you not remember me telling you that he has recently returned from a spell in India?"

She could well have mentioned it amongst all the talk of bonnets and bombazine. "Of course," he lied.

Miss Smythe gestured to the gentleman with wavy black hair and ridiculous side-whiskers who, upon catching their eye, nodded to the row of chairs at the front.

"Oh, there he is." In her excitement, Miss Smythe hopped about like a bird on a perch. "He did say we should all sit together."

Tristan cleared his throat. "I prefer to sit at the back. I find one can appreciate the melody much more when it is carried through the room."

Miss Smythe's bright smile faded. "Oh. But Mr. Fellows is here alone, and it would be rude not to accompany him now he has gone to the trouble of securing the best seats."

Tristan suppressed a smile. "You and Miss Hamilton may sit with Mr. Fellows. I shall sit elsewhere. Besides, I find Haydn can best be appreciated when there are no pretty distractions."

The lady blushed. "Well, if you're sure you don't mind."

"Not at all." He inclined his head. "And poor Mr. Fellows looks as though he could do with some company. Now, make haste before someone attempts to steal the seats from under his nose."

Miss Smythe gasped at the suggestion. "Shall we all meet for refreshments in the interval?"

"Certainly," he said with an affected smile.

Tristan watched them hurry away before heading to the empty row at the back. Dropping down into the chair, he gazed over the sea of heads and stifled a yawn.

Good Lord.

What the hell was he doing?

With each passing day, he lost sight of the man who spied on smugglers, got drunk on cheap wine, cursed and laughed with labourers and farmhands. He hated behaving like a preened prig. Had his mother not been so distraught over the death of his brother, they would be sharing a few stern words.

Tristan closed his eyes, but the low hum of mumbled whispers from the crowd, interspersed with a few strained chords of the cello, proved too distracting. He peered between the rows of shoulders to see Miss Smythe seated next to Mr. Fellows. Perhaps the gentleman had developed an affection for her. Tristan sincerely hoped so as it would ease his burden a little.

As the musicians began to play and the haunting notes filled the air, a sudden shiver raced through his body. Having chosen not to sit next to the aisle—if he fell asleep there was a good chance he would end up on the floor—he was surprised to find that the latecomer had decided to sit next to him as opposed to the empty row adjacent.

For fear of appearing rude he did not gape but glanced covertly out of the corner of his eye. The lady was dressed in grey silk, the edges of her sleeves trimmed with black lace. She held her hands demurely in her lap. The sight of her black gloves, coupled with her sombre-looking gown, complemented his choice of black attire.

The lady edged a little closer.

The air around them vibrated with a nervous energy that had nothing to do with the music. The hairs at his nape stood to attention, his body growing more acutely aware of the woman seated at his side. He shuffled back in the chair in an attempt to study her profile. But without any warning, she spoke.

"Hello, Tristan." Her words were but a soft purr. The soothing sound caused tingles to spark suddenly in various parts of his body, like fireworks shooting and bursting sporadically in the night sky.

He would know her voice anywhere.

He had heard it in his dreams too many times to forget its sweet timbre.

Turning slowly in a bid to prepare his weak heart, he glanced at her face. Her deep pink lips were just as full as he remembered. Her dark brown eyes still held the power to reach into his soul. The ebony curls were just as dark as the night he had covered her body with his own to claim the only woman he had ever wanted.

"Isabella." Years of torturous agony hung within that one word, years of longing, years of living with her betrayal.

"I must speak to you," she said, her breath coming as quick as his.

6

He suppressed a snigger of contempt. She'd had nothing to say to him when she left him and married another man. During the five years since their separation, she could have written to him many times. She could have found him in France if that was what she'd wanted.

Why here?

Why now?

"After all this time, I doubt there is anything left to say." His tone was deliberately cold, blunt. The memories of her were like painful wounds that refused to heal and so he had no choice but to hide them beneath bandages of indifference.

"I did not come here for the music," she whispered, but he noted anger infused her tone.

What the hell did she have to be angry about?

The gentleman in front turned his head. "Shush."

Tristan cast him an irate glare. "And I did not come here to revisit the past," he muttered to her through gritted teeth.

"But this is not about the past." She gave a weary sigh as though she would rather be anywhere else than sitting talking to him. "This is about Andrew."

"Andrew?" He could not hide his surprise.

During the two months since his return, she had not called at the house. She had not come to pay her respects or offer her condolences.

"I cannot speak about it here," she said as she placed a hesitant hand on his arm. His traitorous body responded immediately as a familiar warmth travelled through him. "My carriage is waiting outside."

Without another word, she stood and walked out through the door.

His heart lurched. The urge to run after her would never leave him.

He should tell her to go to the devil, let her husband be the one to listen to her pitiful woes. Turning back to face the musicians, he closed his eyes in the hope the melody would ease his restless soul. But the haunting harmony only served to remind him of all he had lost.

Perhaps if he went to her, she would offer an explanation for her lies and deceit. Perhaps then he would be able to move forward, take a wife and produce an heir.

Straightening his coat as he stood, he crept out of the room.

When it came to Isabella, he would always be too weak to resist.

# CHAPTER 2

*I*sabella Fernall flopped down into the carriage seat and exhaled deeply. Her heart pounded so loudly in her chest the thumping echoed in her ears. She did not need to put her fingers to her cheeks to know they flamed berry red. Besides, how could she when sitting on her hands was the only way to stop them from shaking?

She glanced at the empty seat opposite, at the closed carriage door. Her vague plea had failed to rouse Tristan's enthusiasm. After noting the contemptuous expression on his face, she doubted he would come. Whilst he grieved his brother's passing, the men had never been close. She did not know or understand why. During the last few years, and until his untimely death, Andrew had been a good and loyal friend to her.

The sudden tap on the window made her jump and gasp for breath.

Good Lord. The ghostly hauntings at Highley Grange had turned her into a shivering wreck. Sucking in a breath, she leant forward and opened the door. Catching a glimpse of the gentleman's golden hair and black coat, she sat back in the seat in a bid to compose herself before he entered her conveyance.

9

With swift efficiency, Tristan climbed inside the carriage and slammed the door.

Time stopped. Just for a moment.

He sat down opposite, his glacial gaze scanning the interior as though he would rather observe the quality of the leather than look at her.

"What is this about?" His blunt tone sliced through the air.

In her mind, she imagined slapping the sour look from his face. "It is about your brother." Her reply was equally cold and direct.

He sat back in the seat, folded his arms across his chest and stared right through her. "What could be so important you would wait two months before approaching me? You could have called at the house rather than accost me at a concert."

She searched his face, struggling to find the kind and care-free man who had once stolen her heart. Hostility did not come naturally to him. It was an ill-fitting mask, worn to hide his true feelings.

"I'm sure you know the answer to that," she said haughtily, refusing to let his frosty tone penetrate her composed demeanour. "I tend only to call where I know I will be welcome."

He raised an arrogant brow. "As family, you are always welcome at Bedford Square."

"Family?" She could not help but give a contemptuous snort. "Was I ever anything more than your father's ward? We are not related by blood, and you once said that two summers spent living under the same roof hardly quantifies such a connection."

"My father promised your mother he would care for you, and he was true to his word. You should have made some attempt to repay his kindness by calling on my mother in her hour of need."

Bitterness dripped from every word. Good Lord. Had it not been for the mop of golden hair and the dimple on his chin, she would not recognise him.

"Perhaps you should consult your mother before condemning others," she said in a superior tone. His arrogance was infectious. "I believe she is not of the same opinion when it comes to who she permits entrance into her home." Indeed, Lady Morford had written to her and specifically asked her to stay away.

"You could have asked to speak to me." He examined his fingernails as though he found the conversation highly tedious. "My mother does not dictate whom I see."

"Really? I hear Miss Smythe is your mother's current lady of choice and that you have been instructed to stop and pet her whenever she holds up her paw."

Isabella regretted the words as soon as they'd left her lips. She was not a bitter or resentful person. She did not parade around the ballrooms partaking in spiteful gossip. All she asked for was a little consideration. It took a conscious effort to suppress the pain of the past. She would not have approached Tristan had there been any other option.

"As I said, my mother may do as she pleases. Her actions have no bearing on my decisions."

Isabella sighed wearily. Trading quips with him proved mentally exhausting. That was not the reason she had asked to speak to him. "Then let me take this opportunity to express my condolences for your loss. Indeed, I shall miss Andrew terribly and would have come to pay my respects had I thought I would be welcome."

He straightened, his countenance remaining rather stiff. "I assumed your lack of compassion stemmed from your feelings towards me. I had no idea you were so fond of Andrew."

It hadn't always been the case. She had despised Andrew for the part he'd played on the night she had eloped with Tristan. But he had reached out to her when Lord Fernall died, and she had been so desperately short of friends. Indeed, she would never sully Andrew's memory because of her feelings over Tristan's shortcomings.

"He was there for me when I needed him," she said solemnly. "He was there for me when I had no one else to turn to."

Tristan snorted. "Well, he always knew what to say to win a lady's affection."

*Do not retaliate. That is what he wants.*

"Yes." She smiled as she remembered Andrew's words of reassurance when she told him how frightened she was of living alone at Highley Grange. "He also knew what to say to bring a lady comfort."

Tristan dragged his palm down his face and sighed. "Well, I am pleased he proved helpful to one of us." His tone conveyed a trace of sincerity. It was the first time since the moment she'd sat next to him at Lady Mottlesborough's concert that he sounded somewhat like the man she remembered.

She had expected him to offer another cutting comment and had prepared a response accordingly. Now she did not know what to say. Plunged into an awkward silence, she took the opportunity to examine her feelings.

Tristan was the love of her life.

She supposed she would always love him. One did not give themselves to a man they presumed would be their husband and feel nothing. But the flaming passion she'd once felt in her chest no longer burned with any intensity. Her heart did not skip a beat at the thought of his touch. The desperate ache to be near him, the long, endless hours of agony while she waited to hear his voice, had all abandoned her, too.

Now, there was nothing left but a cold, empty shell.

In those wistful hours before sleep, she often imagined loving another man. It would not be an intense, all-consuming passion. It would be a different sort of love: a shared appreciation for life, a mature feeling of warm companionship and mutual respect.

"I hear your sister has married and moved to Ripon," she

said, deciding it was childish to be bitter and to dwell on an incident that happened so long ago. One of them had to offer the proverbial olive branch. And whether she liked it or not, she needed his help.

"Catherine prefers a life with few distractions. She has never been one for pomp and ceremony."

Isabella understood completely. "And you have spent the last five years in France."

He sat back, his shoulders relaxing a little. "I would still be there now if I had my way." A faint smile touched his lips, and his blue eyes sparkled. For a brief moment she caught a glimpse of the man with whom she had fallen in love. "The monastery is the only place I feel at peace."

"The monastery?" She could not hide her surprise. Had he spent all those years living with monks? "Surely you don't mean you stayed there, that you lived in seclusion, prayed for hours every day."

"Of course not." He offered a mocking snort. "I have never been the pious type. The religious community who once occupied the monastery abandoned it long ago. My good friend Marcus Danbury purchased the property. We were in business together. We had the same goals, the same ideals. Our work proved fulfilling."

"Work?" Isabella shook her head. "But you are the son of a viscount, a viscount yourself now. Why would you have a need to work?"

He did not reply immediately. There was a flash of uncertainty in his eyes before he said, "It is of no consequence. Andrew's death forced me to leave a place I regarded as my home. And so I had no choice but to give up a life I found satisfying."

It suddenly occurred to her that he could not possibly be the same man she once knew. They had spent five years apart, separated by the sea, the language, by circumstance. During that time had he known love, heartbreak? What events had shaped and moulded his character? Would anything else ever compare to the level of satisfaction he had experienced elsewhere?

"The title and land are yours whether you reside in London or not," she said. In his youth, he had been a little reckless. He'd thought nothing of disobeying his family then. "You should follow your heart rather than what society expects or your position dictates."

His expression darkened. "Do you truly believe that? When people depend on us, how can we ever be free? I'm afraid duty and responsibility are hats I must learn to wear comfortably and with pride."

"You sound so different from the man I used to know." The words fell from her lips without thought or censure. She sucked in a breath, wishing they would somehow find their way back. "What I mean is maturity alters the way we view the world. We have come to realise our options are limited."

He snorted in both amusement and mockery. "Indeed, life no longer feels like a glorious adventure filled with endless possibilities."

Isabella sighed. Whilst she recognised the truth to their words, a part of her wanted to kick off her slippers, take his hand and run through the garden like they used to do. The moon would be full and bright. They would sit by the fountain, splashing water, laughing. He would kiss her beneath a blanket of heavenly stars. Life would be perfect, just as it was then.

Good Lord. She was but three-and-twenty, yet she suspected every new experience awaiting her would fall hopelessly short of that one magical night. A surge of raw emotion sought to draw all the air from her lungs. She put her hand to her mouth, coughed against her gloved fingers.

"Listen to us." A weak chuckle left her lips. "We sound so miserable, so morbid."

He stared at her for a moment, the tightness around his jaw

relaxing somewhat. "In France, my friends often remarked on my cheerful disposition. I am known for my optimism, for my carefree attitude to life. Yet I do not recognise myself when I am here. The words that fall from my mouth sound foreign to me. Everything feels like a lie."

Isabella felt a familiar tug in her chest upon hearing his honest words. In an instant, she was transported back to the night at the coaching inn, when they realised it was his father's carriage rumbling into the courtyard. She had put her hand on his cheek, told him nothing would ever keep them apart. Their ability to be honest and speak so openly to one another was just one of the things she loved about being with him.

How ironic that he should deceive her but a few hours later.

"It can take time to settle after years of living a different life," she said, though she wanted to say that she understood what it was like to deceive oneself, that her life had been one huge lie, too. "Things are bound to feel strange, certain modes of conduct uncomfortable."

He narrowed his gaze. "You always did know what to say in any given situation. It is one of the things—" He stopped abruptly, waved his hand in the air. "The more we converse, the further we seem to stray from the original point." His tone was somewhat sharper. "You said you wished to speak to me about Andrew. Am I to assume it was to pay your respects privately?"

Isabella watched him draw back behind a solid wall of ice, a defensive manoeuvre that sent a frosty chill rushing through her.

"Whilst I grieve for Andrew that is not why I was compelled to come here this evening."

He shrugged. "Then what forced you to seek me out?"

Sucking in a breath and squaring her shoulders, she said, "I believe your brother's death was not accidental. I believe someone murdered him."

Tristan jerked his head back as though reeling from a hard

ADELE CLEE

slap. "You believe Andrew was m-murdered?" He gulped and
swallowed deeply. "Why on earth would you think that?"

The story was far too complicated to condense into a
sentence or two. "I cannot explain it now. But say you will meet
me tomorrow in Hyde Park, and I will tell you everything."
Panic flared. She flew forward, put a hand on his arm. "You are
the only person I can turn to for help."

He stared at her black glove as though it was something
foreign to him, something dirty and tainted. When his brows
knitted together and a look of disdain flashed in his eyes, she
knew he did not believe her.

"Andrew is dead," he said bluntly. "Nothing I can do or say
will bring him back." He shuffled to the edge of the seat,
wrapped his fingers around the handle on the carriage door. "I
suggest you speak to your husband if you are in need of attention, for I cannot think of a single reason why someone would
wish to hurt my brother."

Isabella gaped at him as he opened the door and vaulted
down to the pavement.

He struggled to look at her. "If I've any hope of being happy
here, I must move forward. I cannot revisit the past. I'm sure you
understand." Without another word, he closed the door.

The clip of his shoes faded into the distance.

Isabella sat back in the seat as she struggled to make sense of
her chaotic thoughts. She should have explained the catalogue of
mysterious events before revealing her suspicions. Still, the mere
mention of murder failed to rouse his curiosity. Indeed, he had
implied she was somewhat dramatic, perhaps even deceitful.

How hypocritical of him.

He didn't trust her. Their history obviously still weighed
heavily on his mind. Perhaps he'd suspected she was the one
responsible for informing his father of their elopement. Perhaps
he'd doubted her desire to marry him and thought she had used

16

any means necessary to avoid the match, and that had been the reason behind his sudden change of heart.

Something else troubled her, too.

Why would he tell her to speak to her husband?

How could he not know that Lord Fernall was dead?

# CHAPTER 3

"*H*ave no fear," Matthew Chandler said, slapping Tristan playfully on the back. "You'll find no desperate debutantes here. There's no need to scurry behind potted ferns in a bid to hide from matchmaking matrons. Trust me. Any virgin seen stepping through my door is sure to find their reputation in tatters come the morning."

Tristan smiled as he let the decadent atmosphere soothe his anxious spirit. "There are some who would frown at the mere mention of me attending a masquerade so soon after Andrew's death."

He glanced around the ballroom, at the array of vibrant and somewhat indecent costumes, feeling rather more cheerful than he had of late. A few entertaining hours spent in Chandler's townhouse was just what he needed. And his black domino afforded a certain anonymity.

"Propriety is not something my guests are overly concerned with." Chandler's green eyes shone with amusement. "You should make the most of the relaxed modes of decorum. Indulging one's desires is a sure way to ease a troubled mind, my friend."

WHAT YOU DESERVE

Tristan had no intention of conducting an illicit liaison. He was simply grateful not to have Miss Smythe hanging from his coattails. "I was expected to attend Lady Padmore's soiree, but I would prefer to stick pins in my eyes than endure another evening of fake smiles and mindless drivel."

"I still don't understand why you came home." Chandler sighed. "Why give up your happiness just so an heir, which you have yet to produce I might add, can enjoy a life of wealth and prosperity long after you are dead. Spend it all now. That's what I say. Live every day as though it could be your last."

Tristan snorted. He admired Chandler's honesty and relaxed attitude, but their circumstances were entirely different. "Your brother is still very much alive, possesses good business acumen, is sensible enough to ensure your mother and sister never need go without. Your uncle dotes on you, pays your tailor's bills and the repairs to your carriage. If you were forced to take your brother's place, would you still host your exclusive parties then?"

Chandler shook his head. "Good Lord. You have been spending far too much time with your mother. Worrying is not good for the constitution. You'll be grey and wrinkled before you reach thirty." He draped his arm around Tristan's shoulder and stared out over the crowded room. "You see all these people dancing, drinking and making merry. Everyone in here, bar you, has paid for the privilege." Chandler chuckled. "Since Lord Delmont decided to retire from hosting his scandalous balls, I have been inundated with requests for membership. This is an exclusive club of sorts. Uncle Herbert hasn't had to put his hand in his pocket for months."

Tristan envied any man who had the courage and the where-withal to live as he pleased. "Then I commend your efforts. But let me ask you a question. What will you do when you meet a woman you admire, one who disapproves of what you do here?

Would you turn your back on a life of decadence and debauchery? Would you give it all up for love?"

"Love?" he scoffed. "I imagine love to be akin to madness, and I have no desire to spend my days in Bedlam." Chandler brushed his mop of black hair from his brow. "Thankfully, I'm a man incapable of expressing sentiment. However, should such an unlikely occasion arise, I shall just have to hope she's an heiress willing to trade money for aristocratic lineage."

Tristan laughed. It was refreshing to spend time with someone with such loose morals.

"Come," Chandler continued. "I'll not leave you alone to wilt like a wallflower in the corner. If we cannot find a woman to spark your interest, we will drown your sorrows in a bottle of brandy."

Tristan was about to surrender to his friend's profligate suggestion when he noticed Chandler's footman waving at them from the stairs. "It appears your footman wishes you to acknowledge him. Either that or he is so happy in his employment he wants the whole world to know."

"Do I detect a hint of humour?" Chandler gave him a friendly elbow in the ribs. "See. You are beginning to sound more like your old self by the minute."

After witnessing an exchange of nods and odd hand gestures, Tristan watched the footman return to his post. "I assume you could make sense of his ticks and twitches."

Chandler nodded. "Of course. We have an interloper at the door. A lady seeking admittance. My footmen know not to turn away such a ravishing beauty for something as trivial as lacking an invitation."

"How do you know she's a ravishing beauty?" Tristan asked, somewhat baffled.

"It is simple," Chandler informed. "When Dodson touches his finger to his cheek, that means she is beautiful. When he pats his chest, that means she has the assets required to tempt a man to sin."

"Good Lord." Despite the licentious nature of the conversation, Tristan found it far more interesting than talk of ribbons and pins. "So have you given Dodson permission to let her in?"

"You should know I would never want a lady to leave here dissatisfied." Chandler raised an arrogant brow. "It would be disastrous for my reputation. Now, don't tear your gaze away from the stairs. Our beauty is about to make her entrance. Perhaps it might be my lady love, my heiress come to save me from a life as a dissolute rake."

Tristan did not envy anyone forced to make a late appearance. To descend a flight of stairs whilst a hundred pairs of eyes searched for every flaw or imperfection required a certain amount of courage.

He stood next to Chandler and watched with interest. The blood pumped through his veins at far too rapid a rate. The hairs at his nape jumped to attention. He felt excited, alive.

It felt so damn good.

As the mysterious beauty came through the double doors at the top of the stairs, Tristan sucked in a breath. Dressed in a close-fitting black silk gown, her face obscured by a black jewelled mask, the lady was utterly captivating.

"Most people believe black to be a morbid colour," Chandler said, his eyes fixed on the lady before them. "Some would say it is rather dull and uninspiring. But I say it creates an air of wickedness, an element of intrigue that speaks to the hearts of men."

Tristan stared. "Hearts? Are you certain that is the word you wished to use?"

"Watch how she scans the crowd," Chandler said, his rich tone conveying the fact he found the sight highly stimulating. "Watch how she holds her neck defiantly, a warning to those who dare to question her right to be here."

"Do ... do you know her?" Tristan struggled to force the words from his mouth.

Chandler turned to look at him, his brows drawn together. "Are you telling me you don't? If so, I suggest you look a little closer. Indeed, her attendance here tonight is not a coincidence." He turned his attention back to the lady on the stairs, rubbed his chin and said, "How interesting."

Tristan blinked, narrowed his gaze and stared beyond the glittering mask and rouged lips. Her ebony hair was tied back in a loose knot at her nape. The style was simple. It reflected a relaxed attitude, a lack of vanity so opposed to the sensual aura she radiated. As he noted the narrow shape of her chin, the creamy hue of her skin, he felt the familiar tightening in his abdomen that only ever occurred with one woman. Whilst her eyes were hidden behind the delicate mask, he would stake his life that they were a dark chocolate brown.

"Isabella." He had not intended to say her name out loud.

"Indeed," Chandler said with a hint of intrigue.

"What the bloody hell is she doing here?" Only one thought took prominence. Had she come to meet a lover? Jealousy slithered through him.

Chandler cast him a look of disappointment. "What do you think she's doing here? Lord above, all that time spent sleeping with monks has affected your brain."

"I was not sleeping with monks," he snapped. He was not sleeping with anyone.

"Do not underestimate the power of the pious." Chandler chuckled. "Their holy essence lingers in the shadows waiting to numb the senses of unsuspecting gentlemen."

"Have no fear on that score. I am immune." Tristan snorted. Chandler would be shocked to learn of all the things he had done whilst working for the Crown. "During my time in France, I committed many sins against the Lord. All in the name of justice, of course."

His work with Marcus Danbury had resulted in countless fights and brawls, often with pistols and swords, occasionally resulting in death. His wild escapades had moulded his character, made him the man he was today. Not the preened, pretentious prig he saw in the mirror, but the man strong enough to fight for a cause.

"Well, I'm somewhat pleased to hear you finally found the courage to seek refuge in another woman's arms."

Tristan turned to him. He could not suppress the dark cloud descending. "There has never been anyone else. It has always been Isabella."

"Holy heaven." Chandler rubbed the back of his neck and exhaled. "There is a small part of me that is curious to know what it feels like to be that obsessed with a woman. Do you sleep at night? Does the intense feeling of longing ever subside?"

"No."

"Good Lord! Then you're in need of more than a drink."

Tristan watched Isabella hovering on the opposite side of the room, waiting to see who she spoke to, but he struggled to keep her in his line of sight. "What is she doing here, Matthew?" He sighed as he brushed his hand through his hair. But the sudden urge to protect her grew fierce. "Lord Fernall is a blasted idiot. Why would he allow her to venture out on her own at night?"

"I'm confused," Chandler said. "Are you speaking of her stepson? It does sound ludicrous that I should refer to Henry as such when they are practically the same age."

Tristan frowned. "I was not speaking of Henry Fernall, but of her husband."

Chandler slapped his hand to his chest and stepped back. "Her husband?" he repeated. "But Lord Fernall is dead. Surely you knew."

There was a moment of stunned silence.

Tristan repeated the words over and over in his mind for fear he had misheard.

"Dead!" Tristan shook his head. "But you must be mistaken. My mother would have told me." He had seen Henry Fernall at the theatre, but in the crush they had not had a chance to speak. "Someone would have mentioned the fact."

Chandler shrugged. "People probably assumed you knew. As did I."

Tristan stared out across the sea of heads to find Isabella still standing alone. Why the bloody hell hadn't she mentioned it when she'd asked to speak to him in her carriage? Whilst he was annoyed that she had not had the decency to offer her condolences for Andrew's death, he was guilty of the same crime.

An odd feeling of panic flared. "Has she remarried?"

"No. She has been a widow these last two years."

"Two years!" Instant relief was marred by shock. Two blasted years and no one saw fit to write to him in France. His mother had some explaining to do. Andrew hadn't written to him, either. Tristan had always suspected his brother admired Isabella. Perhaps he had thought to use the opportunity to press his advances. Was that why she spoke of him so highly?

"Forgive me. I would have found a more tactful way to tell you had I known." Chandler glanced across the ballroom. "That is why I was surprised you questioned her motive for coming here."

"So she does have a lover then." He hadn't thought the words would sound so bitter.

"No!" Chandler gave a humorous snort. "She is obviously here to see you."

"But I told no one of my intention to attend this evening."

"Then she must have followed you here." Chandler's roving eye ventured to two ladies hovering a few feet away. One was dressed as a shepherdess, the other in a grey nun's habit, though her bold grin suggested her true character was far removed from the one she displayed. "Go and speak to her. I'm sure I can find something to occupy my time whilst you're gone."

The ladies whispered to one another, smiled seductively and then exited through the doors leading out onto the terrace.

"Unless you would prefer a little light relief," Chandler continued. "You're welcome to accompany me on a stroll through the garden. I hear one can often find all sorts of delightful creatures lingering in the shrubbery."

"Your generosity knows no bounds," Tristan said, failing to suppress a grin. He had always found Chandler highly amusing. "But with your gargantuan appetite, I know it will be impossible for you to share."

Chandler slapped him on the back. "You're right, of course. I was simply being polite." As Tristan moved to step away, Chandler caught his arm. "You know there are some who believe Lady Fernall murdered her husband. I'm not one of them, though I wouldn't blame her under the circumstances."

Without another word, Chandler left him alone with his thoughts. Circumstances? What circumstances? Chandler's words hinted at something unpleasant. Anger flared. He would have murdered the man himself if he had proved to be abusive.

Suddenly overcome with a desperate need for answers, he craned his neck in a bid to locate her. Through the boisterous throng their gazes locked. Perhaps she had come to see him after all. Tristan pushed and shoved his way through the crowd in a bid to reach her. Upon witnessing his approach, she straightened and stepped forward.

"Tristan."

"Isabella." He inclined his head. "I am surprised you recognised me whilst I'm wearing a mask."

"I would know your sculptured jaw and dimpled chin in a crowd of a thousand men." The corners of her rouged lips curved up into a half smile. "I see you still find Mr. Chandler's company entertaining."

"I have always admired honesty as opposed to the feigned modes of conduct one witnesses on a daily basis. Chandler speaks his mind, and so I find him rather refreshing."

"Then perhaps we should follow Mr. Chandler's example." She glanced to her left. The couple next to her had forgotten their manners, forgotten that in society one did not squeeze a lady's buttocks without fear of the consequences. Isabella swallowed visibly. "While it is obvious why a gentleman would wish to attend Mr. Chandler's quaint little party, I presume you are wondering what brings *me* here."

He was. But a far more pressing question fell from his lips. "Why did you not tell me Lord Fernall was dead? How is it I am the only person in London not to know you're a widow?"

"I did not tell you because I presumed you knew." She raised her chin though her stained lips trembled slightly. "I thought you still harboured ill feeling towards me and so chose not to mention it."

Damn right he harboured ill feeling.

"I am not so cold and heartless that I would not have sent word to you." Indeed, what would he have done had he known? He'd have been torn between wanting to offer his assistance and wallowing in satisfaction.

She stared at him for a moment. The faint line on her brow was the only sign that she doubted his words. "My husband died two years ago. The precise nature of his death is not something I wish to discuss in public."

"Did you kill him?" He was not surprised by her sharp gasp. His mask afforded him the opportunity to be overly direct. He was glad of it. Living with the knowledge of her deceit had eaten away at him, and he refused to be her fool again.

"How can you ask me that?" She wrapped her gloved fingers around his wrist and pulled him further into the corner. "Regardless of what happened between us, surely you know I could never do such a thing."

He did not have to glance down to know she still gripped his arm. Her touch always soothed him. He often felt like one half of a puzzle: not quite whole, lacking something he could not define. The sudden euphoria upon connecting with the other half stole his breath.

"I want to believe you," he said. She had duped him once before. "But accidents happen. I have known people who have been forced to act violently in order to survive." He thought of Anna Sinclair and her dealings with the mysterious comte. Had Isabella suffered abuse at the hands of her husband?

"Samuel never hurt me," she clarified. "Not in the physical sense." Her gaze shot to a point beyond his shoulder. "We cannot talk here. Walk with me, out in the garden. When you have heard all I have to say, then you may decide if you wish to help me."

"Help you? Help you do what?"

She sucked in a deep breath. "I must find out who murdered my husband, for the same person surely murdered Andrew. Because I believe the same person is now haunting me."

## CHAPTER 4

"*H*aunting you?" Tristan's eyes grew wide in a look of utter disbelief. "What on earth do you mean?"

"Shush." She tapped her finger to her lips. She could trust no one. "Give me your arm. We shall stroll around the garden and take some air."

Isabella breathed a sigh when he inclined his head. Entering Mr. Chandler's house was a risk she'd had no option but to take. People would make assumptions. They would presume her desire to seek the company of dissipated gentlemen was indeed a motive for her to have murdered her husband.

Tristan raised a brow. "If we are recognised or discovered walking out in the garden alone we may find ourselves party to gossip." Despite his cautionary tone, he held out his arm. He appeared more relaxed. No doubt Mr. Chandler possessed the skills necessary to penetrate his stone façade.

"Well, widows are known to be a little lax when it comes to morals." She tried to sound amused, indifferent. "I have been whipped by vicious tongues many times." The years had not made her immune to the pain, but she did not want to give him a reason to refuse. "You are yet to make any formal declaration to

28

Miss Smythe. So, neither of us should have any cause to explain our being here."

Placing her hand lightly in the crook of his arm, she waited for the sudden flutter of excitement in her stomach. It did not materialise instantly. It did not materialise at all. Her body felt numb, her heart empty.

"I was thinking only of you," he said. "And I have no plans to make a declaration. Not to Miss Smythe. Not to anyone."

Whilst she found his first comment touching, she chose not to challenge him for his second. It was common knowledge he planned to take a wife. But she did not want to argue with him. In a fit of anger, she would berate him over his failure to keep his promise to her all those years ago. If they had any hope of working together, it must remain in the past.

Navigating the crowd, Tristan led her out onto the terrace. "Perhaps it is not wise to linger here." He gestured inconspicuously to the amorous couple frolicking in the shadows behind the open door.

Listening to the lady's giggling and ragged breathing reminded her of how much she missed feeling loved and adored. And she could not concentrate on the conversation when the sound of happiness reinforced how terribly lonely she had become.

"No," she said softly, "let us walk where we may have some privacy."

A faint smile touched his lips. "I must warn you that we are bound to meet other couples whilst roaming about the grounds."

She forced a reassuring smile. "It would not be a masquerade if we did not stumble upon at least one illicit liaison."

Tristan inclined his head. "Indeed."

They descended the five stone steps and followed the gravel path as far as the fountain. It occurred to her that the ornate object was perhaps too large for the space, but then she remembered the erotic lure of water. The trickling sound soothed the soul. Playful splashes flicked at a partner were often a prelude to something far more sinful. Indeed, she imagined Mr. Chandler lounging on the grass whilst watching a host of naked nymphs bathe in the stone feature.

"Shall we stop here?" Tristan asked. "There is a bench where we might sit."

Her gaze drifted to the stone seat. Did he recall the hours spent sitting together in the garden at Kempston Hall as fondly as she did? Then again, she supposed his suggestion was purely logical. The grass was still damp from an earlier rain shower. Her slippers would be sodden by the time they returned to the ballroom, the black silk forever stained.

With a quick glance back over her shoulder, she nodded. "Perhaps it is best we do sit." She feared her knees would buckle once she spoke of the burden she carried.

Tristan brushed the stone bench with his gloved hand. "There. That should suffice."

"I am not sure where to begin," she said as she sat down. Her heart was beating erratically at the thought of recounting her nightmare.

Sitting down beside her, he removed his domino mask and placed it next to him on the bench before brushing his hand through his mop of golden hair. "Perhaps you should start by telling me how Lord Fernall died and why there are some who believe you are responsible."

She stared into his eyes as she tried to form a reply. *Cerulean blue*. Those were the words she repeated in her mind whenever she struggled to envisage the exact colour of his eyes. Cerulean —as soothing and just as seductive as a deep blue sky in the height of summer.

She shook her head in a bid to focus on her answer.

"I found Samuel lying sprawled at the bottom of the stairs." She tried not to stare into Tristan's eyes when she spoke. If he was to comprehend the terrifying nature of the events, she could not be distracted. "It was three in the morning. I heard him open the door to his chamber, listened to the heavy, sluggish footsteps of a man in his cups or one still hovering in the realm of sleep."

Tristan raised a brow. "You heard him? You did not share a bedchamber?"

The rigid muscles in her cheeks softened, but she could not quite manage a smile. "No, Tristan. We always slept apart."

He raised his chin in response. "I see. Forgive me. Please continue."

"The footsteps came to an abrupt halt. I heard a gasp and then nothing more."

"Did Lord Fernall not cry out? Did you not hear a dull thud to indicate he had fallen down the stairs?"

She shook her head. "Other than a loud intake of breath, I heard nothing."

"And so you went to investigate."

"Yes." It had taken her five minutes or more to rouse the courage, but eventually, she had peered out into the corridor. "I put on a wrapper and crept along the landing. The house was dark. The oak panelling only serves to make it feel even more oppressive, but still I ventured downstairs."

"Did you see anyone else?"

"No. I was but five or six steps from the bottom when I noticed his body and realised he was dead." She shuddered visibly as she recalled his grisly expression. "His face was ashen, the texture a powdery white. His hair practically stood on end. His body lay twisted and contorted like the corkscrew branches of a willow. Over the years, I have seen many distasteful emotions in his eyes, but I have never seen terror."

Tristan shuffled uncomfortably, his clenched jaw a sure sign of agitation. "Had his heart given out? Did the fall kill him?" He gestured to her mask. "Would you mind removing your disguise? I find I cannot concentrate. I cannot absorb what you're telling me when your face is obscured."

His comment dragged her away from the morbid scene back to the present. She wondered if he doubted her account. Did he imagine she would lie about something so horrifying?

"Forgive me. I know when one intends to deceive it is often reflected in the eyes," she said, although she had failed to notice it in Tristan's. Forcing steady fingers, she removed her mask and placed it on the bench next to his. "You only need to look into mine to know I speak the truth."

For some unknown reason, he gave a mocking snort. His assessing gaze drifted over her face, but he chose not to look into her eyes. "What was the cause of death?"

"Samuel suffered a broken neck. Apparently, death was instantaneous."

Tristan rubbed his chin in silent contemplation. "Although you did not hear a sound," he eventually said, "he could still have tripped and fallen. What makes you believe someone murdered him?"

Just thinking about her time at Highley Grange sent shivers rippling through her. "In the two days prior, we experienced various unexplainable events—strange noises, the sound of footsteps pacing the landing in the dead of night. And then there was a spate of accidents. The horse Samuel had ridden for years threw him unexpectedly. He was walking outside when two tiles slipped from the roof, missing his head by mere inches. I believe someone or something forced him from his bed that night and pushed him down the stairs."

Tristan leant closer, his interest in the topic evident. "Something? You cannot mean an animal, which leads me to conclude you mean a …" Even an erratic wave of his hand failed to help him say the word.

"A ghost. A phantom. The spirit of his first wife."

"Surely you're not serious?"

Raising her chin, she attempted to rouse an element of confidence even though she knew her assumptions were evidence of an unstable mind. "I understand it is hard for you to comprehend," she said, noting the way his bottom lip almost touched his chin. "Had our situations been reversed, I would have tried to find a rational explanation for the sinister events. But I have witnessed things, terrible things that defy all logic and reason."

Tristan sat back. "What sort of terrible things?"

"I should start by explaining that we were not at Grangefields, the Fernalls' family home, but at Highley Grange. It is a house Samuel bought for the sole purpose of entertaining, for those times when he wished for privacy to host his sordid parties. Ordinarily, I would not have been permitted to reside there. But Samuel often found it amusing to taunt those closest to him and I believe, that in those last few days, he feared being alone."

A feminine screech sliced through the air, making them both jump to their feet. She grabbed Tristan's sleeve as her frantic gaze scoured the mass of green foliage and tall shrubbery.

*Had the wailing widow followed her to London?*

Tristan placed his hand over hers. "It is nothing to cause alarm. It is just a few amorous guests lurking behind the hedgerow."

The heat from his hand penetrated her gloves. The friendly gesture was remarkably soothing. Indeed, for a moment she almost forgot she was utterly alone in the world.

She was about to speak when Mr. Chandler sauntered out from behind the topiary hedge. A lady in the guise of a shepherdess hung from one arm. A dishevelled nun, wearing a grass-stained grey tunic, clutched the other.

"You were right to decline my offer," Mr. Chandler called out as the trio strolled back towards the house. "When a man is starving, the last thing he ought to do is share his meal."

Tristan turned to her and snorted in amusement. "Chandler is a rogue though I cannot help but like him."

"He does appear to have a certain appeal. I'm sure you

would have preferred to frolic in the bushes with his companions than hear my morbid tale." A pang of jealousy caused a pain in her chest. Rather than feel disgruntled, she welcomed the feeling for it meant her heart wasn't completely dead.

"Whilst I enjoy Chandler's company, we have very different views on courtship."

Once, she had presumed to know Tristan's character. But she would not make the same mistake again. "Well, you do not have to explain yourself to me."

An uncomfortable silence filled the air.

"You were telling me about the terrible things you witnessed at Highley Grange," he eventually reminded her.

A host of inconceivable images flashed into her mind. "Have you ever seen a ghost? Have you ever seen a spectre disappear before your eyes?" The gravity of her situation lent for a more direct approach.

Tristan jerked his head back in astonishment. "No. But I am of the mind that the living are far more terrifying than the dead." He offered his arm. "Shall we walk? It is not a conversation to have whilst people are lingering in the bushes. By its very nature, the topic would see us both locked away in Bedlam."

She threaded her arm through his. They followed the path around the perimeter of the manicured lawn until the music spilling out from the ballroom became quieter, less of a din.

"The living may be more terrifying," she said, "but at least one can form a rational opinion of what they see. With the dead, one cannot apply the same logic." Indeed, she still struggled to find an explanation for what she had witnessed. "I saw an image of a woman dressed in a white shroud. She stood at the end of a long corridor, pointed her bony finger at me and whispered for me to 'get out'. I buried my head in my hands and when I found the courage to look up she was gone. Suppressing all fear and by sheer strength of will, I took a candlestick in hand and wandered down the empty corridor. I checked all the rooms but found no one."

Tristan inhaled deeply. "That does not mean that this woman in white was a ghost. The mind is a precarious thing. Bleak thoughts bring on bouts of melancholy. One's mood can affect one's interpretation."

Was he implying she had imagined the whole thing?

"What, you believe my fragile emotions played some part in how I perceived the situation?"

He glanced heavenward. "Look up at the sky and tell me what you see. Be specific, detailed."

Isabella stared at him for a moment. It was an odd request. But he had listened patiently to her story, and so she chose to afford him a similar courtesy.

She glanced up at the night sky but struggled to concentrate knowing he was watching her. "The sky is dark," she began.

"Be more specific. Describe exactly what you see."

"Very well." She huffed as she craned her neck. "I see a cold black canopy. I see a ... a crescent moon shaped like a farmer's scythe: pointed, sharp, the blade a perfect arch. I see bright stars smothered by dark, ominous-looking clouds."

When she lowered her gaze, he was facing her.

"Then you see sadness and despair," he said, his sorrowful tone evoking those feelings. "Our perception can alter our view of reality. Your mind has convinced you that there are evil spirits at work, and so everything you see is twisted in order to confirm and support your theory."

She shook her head. "But what of the items that disappear from my dressing table? What of the widow's wails that wake me at night? What of the hound? I lie hidden behind the bed drapes imagining the terrifying sight beyond. I know if I find the courage to venture to the window, the beast will be sitting on the grass staring up at me. I know his beady black gaze will lock with mine as he bares his teeth, snarls and growls."

"Isabella." He put a hesitant hand to her cheek. Her throat grew tight, the lump so large she could hardly breathe. It took a tremendous effort not to close her eyes and take comfort from his touch. "I would lay odds the servants are responsible for the pilfering. No doubt the dog belongs to a local farmer. There is no devil at work. A ghost is not responsible for causing your anxiety. But if one considers your husband's death, coupled with these odd events, then the obvious conclusion is that someone did intentionally cause him harm."

"Andrew thought so, too. Now he is dead."

Tristan's hand slipped from her cheek. "Andrew fell off his horse." His tone carried a hint of frustration. "It was an accident. A foolish one perhaps, but an accident all the same."

She raised her chin defiantly. "An accident that occurred within ten minutes of him leaving Highley Grange."

"Highley Grange?" A deep frown marred his brow, and she sensed him withdraw. "But my mother informed me he died on the road near Hoddesdon."

"Yes. The Grange is less than half a mile from Hoddesdon."

Tristan stepped back. He winced, rubbed the back of his neck over and over as though trying to ease an aching muscle. "You're certain of this?"

"A gentleman who was travelling to Cambridge stopped to help him. He took one look at Andrew and knew he had broken his neck." An icy chill ran through her as she recalled the memory. "Choosing not to move the body, he rode to the Grange to fetch help, what with it being the only house on that stretch of road. I sent Sedgewick into Hoddesdon to bring Dr. Monroe."

Tristan dragged his hand down his face. "Andrew was an accomplished rider. Was there any explanation for the accident? My mother has been too distraught to discuss the finer details."

"No. I recall someone mentioned they had found a dead fox on the road. It was suggested the creature startled the horse which consequently led to Andrew falling. His death was ruled an accident. The doctor dealt with everything. He informed the necessary authorities. We were required to give a brief statement. That was all."

Muttering a string of curses, Tristan turned away. "Why the hell has no one told me any of this?" He paced back and forth; the sharp sound of crunching gravel underfoot conveyed frustration.

"I can only assume you're right. Your mother cannot bear to talk about that night." Isabella did not want to revisit the night, either. "Having lost one son, securing an heir seems to be her only focus. Perhaps having something else to think about has helped to ease her grief."

He threw his hands in the air. "Despite the need to protect her feelings and honour her wishes, I will not rest until I know the truth."

The tension thrumming in the air about them was almost tangible.

She so desperately wanted to ease his torment, thought of laying her hand on his chest to calm the heart she suspected thumped wildly within. But she kept her arms close to her side.

"I have not been back to Highley Grange for a month." She could not envisage going back there again. "I'm renting a house in Brook Street and—"

He swung around. "You're unaccompanied whilst here in town?"

As a widow, it was quite acceptable. "I did not want to stay with Henry." Samuel's son and heir regarded her with disdain. He made no secret of the fact he disapproved of her marriage to his father. "And I knew if I wrote to you, you would not travel to see me."

"Perhaps not."

As they had not spoken since the night he had informed her they could only ever be friends, she would not have asked to stay in Bedford Square, either.

"I cannot afford to remain in town indefinitely. I must return h-home—" The sob almost choked her when she tried to suppress the sound. It was selfish of her to cry when he was the one who had lost his brother in so cruel a way. "I know I must go back, Tristan, but I am frightened."

Without a word, he caught her wrist and pulled her to his chest. "I will help you find the person responsible for these crimes," he said as he held her close. "You will go home, and you will live without fear. I promise you that."

The hard shell around her heart splintered and cracked. She closed her eyes and inhaled the spicy masculine scent that made her head spin. She let the heat radiating from his body soothe her cold, tired limbs. Encompassed tightly in his arms was the only place she had ever felt safe.

He stepped back, cupped her face with both hands. "I will help you," he repeated. "We will begin by returning to Highley Grange. Pack your things tonight. In the morning, I will meet you in Hoddesdon, opposite the Blue Boar Inn."

"You're … you're coming home with me?" Isabella swallowed as she imagined them spending their days strolling in the garden, and their nights huddled around the fire.

He nodded. "Mention it to no one."

That would not pose a problem. She had no friends amongst society.

"But what will you tell your mother?"

He shrugged. "I'll say I'm going to Kempston Hall on business."

An overwhelming sense of gratitude swelled in her chest. "Do you mean it? I cannot thank you enough, Tristan. After all that has happened, I never expected—"

He placed his finger on her lips. "Let us not speak of the past anymore. It will only hinder our progress. Let us accept that we share the same goal, accept that we can work together as friends."

There was a time when she would have told him to go to the devil. But she needed him. She always had.

"You do realise that in offering your assistance you could potentially be risking your life."

"We do not know that for certain," he said confidently. There was not even a flicker of doubt in his dazzling blue eyes. "Until we can establish a motive for murder, we cannot be sure of anything."

When he heard the widow wailing, when he saw the bloodhound slobbering, then he might take a different view.

"We should return to the ballroom." She glanced back at their masks lying on the stone bench. "I have much to attend to if I am to leave in the morning."

He inclined his head. "I suggest we meet at nine. There must be at least thirty coaches passing through Hoddesdon every day on their way to Cambridge. I should like to avoid meeting anyone who might recognise me."

"Nine?" She raised a brow. "But you would need to leave London before six. Is that not far too early for you?"

"At the monastery we often rose before dawn. Sometimes we never slept at all."

"Why?" She smiled in amusement. "Was it some form of penance? Were you forced to confess your sins and say your prayers?"

"No, Isabella. We did what we had to do to stay one step ahead of the smugglers and murderers."

# CHAPTER 5

"*I* shall wait opposite the Blue Boar Inn, near the ancient oak tree." Tristan opened the door of Isabella's carriage and waited for her to settle into the cushioned seat.

Anyone listening would have presumed they were planning a secret rendezvous. A lovers' tryst. A frisson of excitement coursed through his veins. The exquisite emotion brought with it a memory of when they had met under an old cedar tree. That afternoon, she had climbed into his conveyance to set out on an adventure, a quest for the freedom to express their love.

"I shall meet you there at nine." She lurched forward, placed her hand lightly on his arm as he held on to the door. "Thank you. Perhaps tonight I might finally be able to sleep."

He forced a smile to disguise the distress her touch evoked. How would he fare spending a few days in her company? When all was done and settled, would she put him out of his misery and explain her reason for marrying Lord Fernall? Would the truth ease years of excruciating torment?

"Until tomorrow." He inclined his head, grateful that his mask concealed any evidence of his chaotic emotions.

"Until tomorrow." She sat back against the squab and gave a curt nod.

Tristan closed the door firmly, called up to the coachman to convey her destination. The carriage lunged forward, picked up a gentle pace. He removed his mask, stood and watched as it turned the corner and disappeared from view. But he continued to stare at nothing for a few moments longer.

The friendly pat on his shoulder jolted him back to the present.

"I must say I did expect you to leave with her." Chandler stood at his side and stared into the distance, too. "You are both free to conduct a discreet liaison."

In truth, he could think of nothing he would rather do. Things would have been so different had they only just met.

"We are friends, nothing more." It hurt to say the words. He wanted to believe them. But something inside refused to acknowledge all hope was lost, refused to accept that was the extent of their relationship. "Everything else is in the past."

"Is it? I'm not so certain."

Tristan whipped around to face him. "She married another man," he said through gritted teeth. He had to unleash his pent-up anger on someone.

Chandler shrugged, unaffected by his volatile mood. "But he is dead, and you are very much alive."

"Am I?" He had been dead inside for five years.

Chandler appeared confused by his reply. "You're letting resentment cloud your judgement."

"Are you telling me you wouldn't feel the same way if you were in my position?"

"I have no notion how I would react. I have never loved a woman the way you love her."

Chandler's words were like a barbed arrow to his heart. Amidst the bedlam of the emotional battle raging inside he tried to make sense of his feelings. He had loved Isabella for as long as he could remember. Whilst bitterness had forced him to suppress the feeling, love still flourished deep within.

"Is it so obvious?" he asked with some amusement. To laugh was just another way of coping.

"You had the opportunity to dally with a shepherdess whose wicked tongue can bring any lost lamb to heel." Chandler raised his hand as a means of preventing any interruption. "Don't say you were only thinking of my interests. There are plenty of ladies here eager to spend time in my company."

"Plenty?" Tristan snorted, although he knew Chandler was never short of female companionship. "You always were a conceited devil."

"There is a vast difference between conceit and confidence." Chandler smiled as he raised a brow. "I am confident in my ability to please. Now, shall I give you some advice?"

Tristan waved for him to continue. "Please do."

"Look beyond what you believe to be true. Ask yourself why a woman would turn her back on the man she loves in order to marry a cold-hearted blackguard."

Was that to be the extent of his friend's wisdom? Tristan had thought about nothing else for the last five years. The permanent pounding in his head was testament to that. "The answer is obvious. She married for money and status. At the time, I was but the second son of a viscount."

"You make it sound as though you were a pauper." Chandler frowned. "Do you truly believe Isabella would have chosen a title and money over love?"

"No. I do not." Tristan closed his eyes briefly as he recalled the moment he learnt of her duplicity. "That is what shocked me most of all."

"I fear not all is as it seems. When a person's actions appear illogical, there is always a vital piece of information that has been overlooked."

Suspicion caused his heart to race. "Do you know something more? Is there something you're not telling me?"

Chandler shook his head. "Of course not. But I excel in observing people and their habits. I know the face of a woman capable of deceit. I know greed. I know the actions of a woman whose interests are purely self-serving."

"But you do not know the face of a woman in love," Tristan countered. "Perhaps I misread her affections. Perhaps she realised it was not love she felt."

Chandler gave a mischievous grin. "I don't want you to think my debauched antics in any way have affected my preferences in the bedchamber, but you are a remarkably handsome man." Chandler gripped Tristan's shoulder and squeezed. "I do not know what you have been doing in France, but I imagine your body resembles the marble statues of Greek gods so often displayed in museums. You're kind and generous, loyal to a fault. What is not to love?"

Tristan laughed, though was somewhat bemused by his friend's compliments. "Had I not known of your voracious lust for women I might have been worried."

"Whilst I often go to great lengths to shock and cause outrage, I come out in an ugly rash whenever I brush against a gentleman's bristly chin."

It had been months since Tristan had laughed so hard. He made a mental note to spend more time with Chandler.

"I am off to Bedfordshire on estate business for a few days, but I have a feeling I may be in need of your company upon my return." Indeed, a few days spent with Isabella was sure to be a torturous affair. "Do you still frequent White's?"

Chandler snorted. "Not since I was a snivelling pup. My tastes tend to lean towards the ruinous. There is a rather adequate sink of iniquity on James' Street. Perhaps you might care to join me there one evening."

Tristan's experiences in France had taught him that gambling was a one-way road to debtors' prison. "I'll accompany you, but only as a spectator. I lack your skill when it comes to card games."

"And my skill with women." Chandler slapped him on the back. "What a shame you're off to Bedfordshire. My advice regarding Isabella was to spend more time in her company. Only then will the truth become abundantly clear." Chandler sighed. "Now, the night is still young. Shall we see if we can find that tempting shepherdess?"

Tristan shook his head. "I'm afraid I must decline. I must rise early in the morning if I'm to make it to Kempston at a reasonable hour."

"Indeed." Chandler gave a knowing smirk. "Well, enjoy your time in Bedfordshire. I certainly hope your business proves fruitful."

～

It was midnight by the time Tristan returned home to Bedford Square, still relatively early by most gentlemen's standards.

"Is Lady Morford in her chamber?" Tristan could not leave London without informing his mother that he had business at Kempston Hall. In the process, there were a few questions he had regarding the death of Lord Fernall.

"No, my lord. Lady Morford is waiting in the parlour. She asked to be informed the moment you returned." Ebsworth waved gracefully at the door to their left. "And a Mr. Fellows is waiting for you in the study."

Fellows? What the hell did he want at such a ridiculous time of night?

"You should have informed him I was not at home." His sharp tone conveyed his irritation.

Ebsworth inclined his head by way of an apology. "Forgive

me, my lord. But Lady Morford insisted I show the gentleman in."

Tristan cursed silently. "Inform Mr. Fellows of my return and explain that I shall attend him shortly." Anyone inconsiderate enough to call at a late hour should be made to wait.

Ebsworth bowed. "Certainly, my lord."

Tristan strode to the parlour. He hovered outside the door to calm his ragged breathing. It would be a mistake to charge into the room and demand to know why the hell no one had told him of Lord Fernall's death. There were many more burning questions, too. Why hadn't she told him Andrew had been visiting Isabella when he died? And what the hell was his brother doing there in the first place?

With a shake of the head, he tapped the door and entered.

"Tristan. Is that you?" His mother lay stretched out on the chaise. In one hand, she clutched a lace-trimmed handkerchief; the other hand lay limply over her brow. "Ah, there you are."

"Is it not a little dark in here?" He glanced at the solitary candle flickering in its holder on the side table. "We have no need to be frugal."

"I find the light hurts my eyes." She gave a woeful sigh.

"Ebsworth said you were waiting for me to come home."

She raised her arm slowly, as though it weighed more than her entire body, and waved her handkerchief. "Help me to sit up, won't you."

Melancholy obviously had a debilitating effect on her. He assisted her in shuffling to an upright position, found a cushion to support her back.

"Mr. Fellows is waiting to speak to you," she said. "He told me that you did not attend Lady Padmore's soiree. Apparently, Miss Smythe was expecting to see you there and was frightfully disappointed to find you absent."

Had Fellows come purely to chastise him for his thoughtless-

45

ness? He suspected the gentleman had only been granted entrance because of his eagerness to speak of Miss Smythe.

"I made no promises to Miss Smythe." Whilst he felt the need for honesty, he did not want to antagonise a lady in mourning. "I decided to visit an old friend. His company proved to be rather entertaining, hence my decision to forgo Lady Padmore's soiree."

His mother's eyelids suddenly appeared less hooded, and she cast him a look that conveyed an inner frustration. "But only two nights ago you left the Mottlesborough concert before the interval without saying a word to Miss Smythe. Your indifferent behaviour will leave a stain on her reputation. What must she think of you?"

Tristan pushed his hand through his hair. "Miss Smythe was in the company of Mr. Fellows. It would have been rude of me to interrupt."

She flapped her pristine white handkerchief. "Well, where did you go?"

"Does it matter?"

"Matter? Good heavens. You left your betrothed in the company of another gentleman, of course it matters." She placed her hand to her chest. "I fear my heart cannot stand the strain."

He was suddenly grateful he had not sat down. To jump out of the chair in a burst of anger would surely bring on one of her migraines.

"Miss Smythe is not my betrothed. Whilst she is quite amiable, I have no intention of marrying a woman who speaks of nothing but sewing."

"Sewing! The lady is accomplished in many things. I'm sure if you went to the trouble of spending an entire evening in her company you would discover that her talents know no bounds." His mother nodded as though agreeing with a comment he had yet to make. "Yes. Yes. You must spend the afternoon with her. Take her for a ride in the park, to Gunter's or wherever you young people go for amusement. I shall send a note and arrange it on your behalf."

Tristan sighed, purely to suppress a smirk. "I'm afraid my afternoon with Miss Smythe will have to wait. I must ride to Kempston as a matter of urgency."

"Kempston? Kempston! How long will you be gone?"

Tristan shrugged. "Three days, assuming all goes well. Perhaps a little longer." He considered journeying to France and saying *to hell* with it all.

"Three days?" Her handkerchief slipped from her fingers as she flapped her hands in annoyance. "Can't Mr. Henderson deal with things? What do you pay the man for if he cannot cope with simple problems?"

"Whatever the problem, I must leave in the morning." It was wrong to distrust one's mother, but he chose not to reveal his time of departure for fear he would wake to find his wrists and ankles tied to the bedposts.

"But you can't go. You're needed here. Our situation is dire. I cannot cope without you."

He refused to let his mother use her grief for Andrew's passing as a means to control him. "I am needed at Kempston Hall," he reiterated firmly. It crossed his mind to broach the subject of Lord Fernall's death, but he did not wish to rouse her suspicions.

"And what am I to tell Miss Smythe when she calls tomorrow afternoon to take tea?"

Tristan coughed into his fist to suppress a chuckle before feigning a serious expression. "Tell her you're interested in the alterations she has made to her bonnet. That way I doubt she'll even notice my absence."


Tristan strode towards the study expecting to feel a wave of guilt for not agreeing to his mother's petty demands. But instead, his

ADELE CLEE

body felt lighter; there was a playful spring to his step, and his wide grin stretched from ear to ear. He hadn't felt this good in months.

With a contented sigh, he entered the study.

Mr. Fellows stood. He had not given Ebsworth his hat. Instead, he held it in front of him, fed the rim back and forth through nervous fingers.

"Mr. Fellows." Tristan inclined his head. "I must admit it is rather late to be making a house call. Luckily, I am in a good mood. Now, what can I do for you?"

"Forgive the intrusion, my lord. I know we have not been introduced, but I am recently acquainted with Lady Morford, and am here on an errand of sorts."

Tristan raised a brow. "An errand? Given the hour, I assume it is a matter of considerable importance." Under any other circumstances, he would have been intrigued, had he not known Mr. Fellows enjoyed playing nursemaid to Miss Smythe.

"I suppose it could have waited. But when my mind is occupied, I find I simply must act."

"As we are barely acquainted, I assume you speak on behalf of another." He did not have time to waste and so chose to come directly to the point.

"Indeed." Mr. Fellows prised his fingers from his hat and brushed a hand through his wild mop of black hair. "I wish to discuss Miss Smythe, though she is unaware of my presence here."

Tristan waved for him to sit. The night had brought many strange and shocking revelations, and he needed a drink. "Would you care for refreshment?" he said, gesturing to the range of crystal decanters on the side table. "Brandy or port?"

"I'm afraid I must abstain." Mr. Fellows perched on the edge of the chair. "But please, do not refrain on my account."

Tristan poured himself a drink and dropped into the chair opposite. "Now, have you come here to chastise me for my treat-

48

ment of Miss Smythe or to enquire as to my intentions towards her?"

Mr. Fellows blinked several times, his expression revealing an element of shock. The muscle in his cheek twitched. "Erm … both."

Tristan raised his glass in salute. "Then let me start by saying I respect your honesty. I suspect your concern stems from an admiration for the lady."

"I find Miss Smythe to be brimming with warmth and grace. She is kind and good-natured and deserves a gentleman who appreciates such attributes."

The gentleman appeared smitten. Tristan knew that feeling well.

"Then let me ease your fears. I find Miss Smythe … enchanting, but I have no desire to pay her court. It is my mother who wishes me to marry. I have yet to give the matter any consideration."

The night was improving rapidly. Mr. Fellows would declare his intentions. His mother would stop pestering him, and Miss Smythe could spend her days talking incessantly about her hobbies.

All he had to deal with now was a potential murderer, a phantom in a white cloak and a wild dog thirsty for blood.

"It … it is out of character for me to be so forward," Mr. Fellows informed. "But I noticed you left the Mottlesborough concert with a lady and hoped your interest lay elsewhere."

A mild sense of panic flared.

Had Fellows found the quartet tedious and let his gaze wander or was it his intention to use a veiled threat to bolster his position?

"The lady is an old friend, nothing more." Tristan did not wish to give him food for the ravenous gossips. He was tired and needed to bring the conversation to an end. "I'll be out of town for a few days. On my return, I shall ensure Miss Smythe understands my position. In the meantime, have my assurance that you may pursue the lady with my blessing."

Mr. Fellows stood. "I thank you for seeing me at such a late hour. I feared a measure of hostility but am pleased you understand my intention is purely to see Miss Smythe happy."

Tristan came to his feet. "As is mine," he said. "I'm conscious that my mother may have coerced the lady into believing we would make a good match, and so my absence will help to provide some clarity." Besides, he had a feeling Priscilla Smythe admired Mr. Fellows greatly.

"Are you off on a jaunt?" the gentleman asked with a hint of enthusiasm.

Tristan gave an indolent wave. "I'm afraid not," he said, walking Mr. Fellows to the door. "I'm away to Bedfordshire on estate business."

Mr. Fellows inclined his head. "Then accept my apologies again for disturbing you at such a ridiculous time of night. And let me say that while one's responsibilities can be rather laborious and mundane, I grant that you may find a modicum of merriment and pleasure."

Tristan suppressed a grin. There was nothing mundane about spending time with Isabella. He wondered what the next few days would bring. Would he learn to forgive her duplicity? Would he experience the sweet taste of her lips once again?

"Thank you, Mr. Fellows," he said feeling eager to retire to his bedchamber, though he doubted he would sleep. "I am hopeful some aspects of my trip will prove pleasing."

## CHAPTER 6

The painted sign of the Blue Boar Inn creaked as it swung violently back and forth on its iron hinge. Despite being nestled safely inside the confines of her carriage, Isabella gripped the seat as a blustering north wind rocked the conveyance.

"Good Lord," she muttered as pebble-sized raindrops pelted the window. For the umpteenth time, she glanced through the viewing pane behind. The road was deserted. The relentless downpour continued to bombard the overflowing puddles. Black clouds threatened thunder. "Oh, Tristan. Where are you?"

A part of her hoped he had stopped to take shelter; it did not matter that he was late. A part of her longed to see his mud-splattered face just to know all was well.

The carriage swayed again. This time, the motion was insti-gated by the coachman whose gruff commands suggested he was struggling to settle the horses.

Lowering the window an inch, she called up to Dawes, "Can we wait a few more minutes?"

"Yes, my lady." Dawes muttered something about the thunder, but she struggled to hear him for his words were whisked away by the wind.

Odd irrational thoughts flitted through her mind. Was the storm an ominous warning to stay away? Were the ghosts of Highley Grange out to prevent her impending return?

The sudden rap on the window made her jump. Her hand flew to her mouth, slipped to her chest when she realised it could be Tristan.

She thrust forward, lowered the pane a fraction more and blinked away the droplets of water. "Tristan?"

The figure perched upon the chestnut stallion wore the collar of his greatcoat high, his hat tilted forward to obscure his face. His commanding presence stole her breath. "How far is it to Highley Grange?"

Isabella would know Tristan's voice anywhere, although she wasn't sure if he was speaking to her or Dawes.

"Less than half a mile, my lord" came her coachman's reply.

Tristan turned to her. Rain poured from the brim of his hat. "Close the window. I'll meet you there."

Without uttering another word, he was gone.

She fumbled with the window, sat back in the seat and exhaled. Tristan would need a hot bath to warm his cold bones, a tonic to keep a chill off his chest. Please God, she hoped he did not come down with a fever. She could not have another man's death on her conscience.

But Tristan was not just any other man.

Despite all that had happened, she could not lose him. To live in a world knowing he was no longer in it would be the end of her.

The carriage lurched forward. The coachman's roars and cries were aimed to encourage the spiritless horses to push through the storm. They rattled on for ten minutes or more before she noticed them slowing, before each revolution of the carriage wheels seemed to take a tremendous effort.

They stopped. Jerked forward. Stopped again.

Her world tipped to the left, her sense of balance thrown off kilter by what she suspected was a wheel stuck in the mud.

Dawes climbed down from his perch and rapped on the window. "We're stuck, my lady," he called through the pane.

Isabella opened the door. "Is it the wheel? Can you not free it?"

Dawes shook his head. "Not on my own, my lady. I need to fetch help."

"How long will it take?" Being a gentleman, Tristan would wait for her to arrive at Highley Grange before entering her home. She could only hope he would take shelter in the stables.

"I can't leave you here, my lady. It could take hours." Dawes groaned and winced as a gust of wind almost took the door off its hinges. "I can free one of the horses from its harness, but there's no saddle."

The sound of a horse's hooves squelching in the mud captured her attention. Tristan appeared, strong and commanding like a knight of old. Dawes stepped back.

"You'll need to come with me." Tristan gripped the reins with one hand and held the other hand out to her. "Do you have a cloak?"

"Yes. Give me a moment." Isabella unfolded the garment lying on the seat next to her, threw it roughly around her shoulders before jumping down to the ground.

Mud oozed around her ankles, and she thanked the Lord she'd worn her sturdy boots.

"Give me your hand. You'll have to sit in front of me." Tristan leant down, wrapped his gloved hand around her forearm and hoisted her up to sit sideways. "Lean into me. Put one arm about my waist." He turned his attention to Dawes. "We'll send someone to you as soon as we reach Highley Grange."

"Yes, my lord."

"You should wait inside the carriage, Dawes," she said,

53

feeling a pang of guilt for leaving the poor man behind in such treacherous conditions.

Dawes straightened the collar of his greatcoat and shrank down into its depths. "I'll stay with the horses, my lady, but I thank you all the same."

A loud clap of thunder roared through the heavens.

"We must go." Tristan urged his horse forward and soon they were cantering along the road.

The wind whipped about them. She gripped on to him with all the strength she could muster. As the rain hit her face with the force of hail stones, she pressed her cheek to Tristan's chest. It didn't matter that his coat was sodden. Somehow it still felt warm and comforting.

They came to the crossroads where the stone memorial stood proudly on the grassy mound. "It's left here, and just a minute or so more."

Another boom of thunder crashed through the sky.

Water dripped from his hat onto her cheek. The droplets trickled down her neck, but still she huddled into him as they continued their journey.

"We're here," Tristan eventually said, his weary sigh breezing over her face as she looked up into his brilliant blue eyes. "Thankfully, the gates are open. My legs feel so numb I doubt I'll be able to climb down."

She had no desire to move. "You'll need a hot bath to ease your stiff muscles," she replied, wishing they had another hundred miles to travel.

They rode up the long curved drive, designed specifically to give the impression that the surrounding land appeared far more extensive than it was in reality.

No one came to greet them.

They stopped in front of the iron-studded door. Tristan held her arm as she slid down to the ground. "Go inside where it is warm and dry. Where will I find the stables?"

"Follow the path round to the left." She shivered as she wiped the running rivulets from her face. Had the damp air finally penetrated or did the coldness she felt stem from the loss of Tristan's touch? "I'll ask Mrs. Birch to heat some water so you may bathe."

An image of them sharing the large metal tub flashed into her mind, but she shook it away along with the drops of rain clinging to her cloak.

"Go inside," he repeated. "I'll join you shortly."

Isabella did as Tristan asked. The front door was unlocked. She strode through the hall, leaving muddy footprints in her wake. Sedgewick was nowhere to be seen. Due to her last-minute decision to return, she had not had an opportunity to send word to her staff.

Following the sound of lively chatter, she made her way to the drawing room to find Mrs. Birch, Sedgewick, the chamber-maid and the footman seated around the card table. She stood in the doorway, water dripping onto the polished wooden floor, and watched with interest.

"You've pulled that one out from your sleeve," the footman grumbled. "There are only four kings in a pack, and we've played them all."

"Are you accusing me of cheating?" Sedgewick said in his usual lofty tone as he raised his chin. "Is that any way to speak to a superior?"

"We've played three," Molly said.

"How would you know?" the footman countered. "You've nodded off twice. There's only one way to know for sure."

"You've more than likely miscounted." Mrs. Birch slapped his hand away from the pile of cards in the centre of the table. "Have you been at my lady's sherry again?"

Isabella stepped into the room. "I certainly hope not as I am in need of more than one glass."

Four heads turned to the door. Their shocked expressions

were quickly replaced with looks of horror. For a few seconds no one moved; no one spoke.

"Lady Fernall," Mrs. Birch finally gasped. The chairs scraped along the floor as the servants shot to their feet. "We were not expecting you home."

"I can see that," Isabella replied with just a hint of irritation. In truth, she was too tired and too wet to care.

Sedgewick inclined his head. "I am afraid I have been led astray, my lady."

Mrs. Birch elbowed the butler. "Let me explain, my lady—"

"You may save your explanations until later." Isabella held out her arms. "As you can see, we were caught in the storm and are soaked to the skin."

Mrs. Birch craned her neck to peer over Isabella's shoulder. "We, my lady?"

"Lord Morford has come to stay for a few days. Let us pray Jacob is in the stables waiting to attend to him and not gallivanting around the countryside jumping fences on my horse."

The housekeeper opened her mouth, snapped it shut, but then said, "Forgive me, my lady, but isn't Lord Morford ... d-dead?"

It suddenly occurred to her that the woman was referring to Andrew. Good heavens, fear might have addled her senses, but she had not lost her faculties.

"It is the gentleman's younger brother who has come to stay. When he returns from the stable, he will require a warm bath and his clothes will need airing. A hot meal and a tonic will help to prevent him catching a chill."

They all raised their chins in acknowledgement.

Mrs. Birch turned to Molly. "The longer he remains in damp clothes the worse it will be."

"Well, what are you waiting for?" Isabella sucked in her cheeks and raised a brow to convey her impatience. "Will someone go and heat the water?"

Molly gasped. After offering a curtsy, she scurried out into the hall.

"Lord Morford will take Lord Fernall's old chamber," Isabella continued, aware of the curious look that passed between her servants. Should Tristan object, she would offer him the choice of another room. But she had her own agenda for making the request. Tristan needed to remain close if he was to bear witness to the strange phenomena. "Light the fire in his chamber and have a bath drawn for him as soon as possible."

They all nodded and hurried from the room. Mrs. Birch hovered at the door. "Won't you need some help to change out of your wet clothes?"

Isabella shook her head. "I shall manage. I would rather you all attend to Lord Morford." If she caught a chill, no one would care. If anything were to happen to Tristan—

Mrs. Birch gave a weak smile. "If you're sure, my lady."

Her housekeeper knew not to pester her. Whilst Isabella had use of the house until she remarried or met her demise, it was Henry Fernall who paid their wages. Henry Fernall was responsible for the running of the estate. Henry Fernall controlled everything.

Samuel knew how to torment her even from the grave.

Highley Grange embodied the romantic aspects of any medieval-inspired building. It was not difficult to imagine a row of archers hiding behind the parapets, or a damsel waving her pristine handkerchief from her room in the ivy-covered tower. Nor was it hard to believe one might see the hazy white figure of a ghost appear in one of the arched windows.

Tristan snorted. He would wager there was a full suit of armour standing guard in the hall, and a pair of crossed swords displayed on the wall in case one was suddenly called upon for battle. The environment lent itself perfectly to a haunting.

The stables appeared to be deserted. Tristan searched the stalls to discover the groom asleep on a mound of hay.

"Does your mistress pay you to lie about idle?" he said, nudging the man with the tip of his wet boot. When that failed to rouse him, Tristan tickled the lazy rogue's ear with a piece of straw and shook a few drops of rain from his hat onto the man's cheek. "Wake up."

The groom woke with a start, slapped his ear as the water ran down his neck. "What? I said I'd have the money on Thursday." He dragged a dirty hand down his face and blinked rapidly. "What? Who are you?"

Tristan did not know whether to let the chuckle fall from his lips or chastise the man for his impudence. Having spent years living in the monastery, Tristan still found that the lines between master and servant were somewhat blurred.

"I am Lord Morford," he said, failing to sound irate. "Now get up before your mistress catches you shirking your duties. Your coachman is stuck in the mud less than half a mile from here and requires assistance."

"Lord Morford?" The man sat bolt upright. His wide eyes flitted back and forth as though he feared he was still lost in his dream. "But you're dead," he said before covering his mouth with his hand by way of an apology for his impertinence.

Tristan sighed. Did everyone at Highley Grange believe in ghosts? "You speak of my brother. Trust me. I am very much alive. Now get up before I drag you up."

"Good Lord," the man muttered, scrambling to his feet. "I mean, my lord. Won't you forgive a man for his stupidity?" He held his hands in front of him and twiddled his fingers. "I was just taking a nap. That was all."

"What's your name?"

"J-Jacob, my lord."

"Well, Jacob. I assume you have a cart here."

"Yes, my lord."

"Good. As I said, the carriage is stuck in the mud. Your coachman hasn't the strength to move it on his own." The groom's confused expression hardly raised confidence in his abilities. "You'll need a rope and a couple more men."

Jacob scratched his head. "Do you know where we'll find him?"

"Past the crossroads on the road into Hoddesdon." Tristan stepped back and gestured for the man to exit the stall. "I suggest you take a piece of board or a few logs, and a shovel."

"Yes, my lord," he said, nodding too many times to count. Jacob rushed towards the stable door but stopped abruptly. "Will you be telling Lady Fernall about my nap?"

Isabella had more important things to think about without hearing about the inadequacy of the hired help. "I tend to judge a man on the quality of his work," Tristan said. "I've left my horse in the end stall. Treat him well and I shall forget I saw you sleeping."

Relief flashed in the groom's eyes. "Thank you, my lord. His coat will be shinier than your boots by the time I'm finished with him."

His boots were sodden and splattered with mud. "Splendid." It suddenly occurred to Tristan that he should take advantage of the groom's willingness to please. Whilst the coachman's need was great, Jacob might not be as forthcoming on his return. "Can I ask you something before you rush off?"

"Yes, my lord."

"It might sound like an odd question, but have you ever witnessed anything unusual here?" He could hardly come out and ask the man if he had ever seen a figure in white wandering the corridors. "Have you ever seen anything that defies all sense and logic?"

"All sense and logic?" Jacob repeated, a look of confusion

marring his brow. He stared at Tristan for a moment. "Oh, you mean a ghost. I have heard some say they've seen a lady walking about at night." He glanced back over his shoulder before taking a step closer. "They say it's the spirit of his lordship's first wife."

"Who said that?"

Jacob shrugged. "Mrs. Birch for one. She's been the housekeeper here for ten years. And then there's Molly, but she tends to agree with Mrs. Birch. Mr. Blackwood says they'll say anything to squeeze another shilling from him."

Tristan raised a curious brow. "Mr. Blackwood?"

"He lives in the gatehouse. He takes care of things, manages the estate, but he spends a lot of his time in London."

In a bid to escape the torrential downpour, Tristan had not paid much attention to the stone cottage next to the gates. "Is Mr. Blackwood here now?"

Jacob shook his head. "I've not seen him about for a few days."

Why would Mr. Blackwood spend time away when he was employed to manage Highley Grange? "Is Lady Fernall aware of his fondness for roaming?"

"Even if she is, I don't suppose it matters. It's Lord Fernall who pays his wages." Jacob sneered. "It's Lord Fernall who pays all our wages."

Not wanting a repeat of their earlier misunderstanding by reminding the groom that Lord Fernall was indeed dead, Tristan said, "I gather you speak of Lady Fernall's stepson."

Jacob nodded.

So Isabella had not inherited the house from her husband else Henry Fernall would not have assumed direct responsibility for the staff.

The sudden rumble of thunder caused guilt to flare. The poor coachman had been left waiting at the side of the road. He had kept the groom far too long.

"Just to clarify before you go, other than what the housekeeper has told you, you have never witnessed any strange occurrences yourself."

"Strange occurrences?" The words came out as one elongated sound. He scratched his head. "I've heard the odd howling noise at night. I've found dead animals buried in the gardens, but there's nothing odd about that … just a fox hiding his secret food store."

It was as Tristan suspected. Depending upon how one chose to perceive a situation, one could easily regard an ordinary everyday event as macabre.

"I thought to find headless knights and persecuted priests haunting an old place like this," Tristan said, feigning amusement.

"I can't say as I have much cause to go wandering about the house. I'd tell you to ask Mrs. Birch, but Mr. Blackwood told her he'd not be happy if he heard her talking nonsense again."

Judging by the anxious look in Jacob's eyes, Mr. Blackwood was a man to be feared.

# CHAPTER 7

It was remarkable how daylight held the power to banish fear. Despite the rain clouds littering the blue sky, it still brought a sense of peace. Staring out over the manicured lawns, Isabella let her gaze drift beyond what was trimmed and preened, up to the rolling meadow in the distance. The landscape filtered from the sublime to the picturesque. The long grass seeded with wildflowers appealed to her free spirit. It reminded her of the last summer she had spent at Kempston Hall. The days had been long, filled with gaiety and laughter. Walks through the meadow with Tristan always culminated in a warm embrace and a chaste kiss. Love blossomed. Her heart soared.

Now, it was but a treasured memory, and she could only imagine the scene from behind a pane of glass.

With some reluctance, she stepped away from her bedchamber window. At night she would not dare to come within three feet of the closed drapes, fearing what she would find. Still, her mind concocted images of savage dogs and ghostly spectres—just to taunt her.

She wandered about her room for an hour, maybe more, until

the sound of a door closing and retreating footsteps drew her attention. The steps were light, measured, those of her footman. A strange fluttering filled her chest at the thought that, at some point during the last hour, Tristan had lounged naked in the bathtub just across the landing.

She sat on the edge of her four-poster bed and stared at the brass doorknob. Why did she feel like a naughty child forbidden to leave her room? How could the thought of having Tristan in her home rouse feelings of anxiety and excitement both at the same time?

One thing was certain. Tonight, sleep would elude her. Fear would play no part in her inability to relax. Instead, she would replay every word spoken the night he broke her heart. Searching for an answer to the conundrum often hurt her head.

Why hadn't she simply asked him for an explanation?

Pride played a huge part. And living in ignorance was often better than living with the truth.

Good Lord! She wanted to slap herself for being so weak and pathetic.

Puffing her cheeks and exhaling loudly, she jumped off the bed and marched to the door. She could not sit in her room for the rest of the day. As mistress of the house, she ought to at least give her guest a tour.

Tugging open the door with a newfound level of determination, she failed to notice Tristan hovering outside. By the time she looked up and met his gaze, her eagerness had given her a boost of momentum, and she barged straight into him.

He wrapped his arm around her waist to steady them both. "I know you're pleased I am here but don't you think jumping into my arms is taking your appreciation a little too far? A simple *thank you* would have sufficed."

Oh, the gentleman knew what to say to unnerve her.

Isabella straightened and stepped away. Feeling a blush rise to her cheeks, she brushed the skirt of her dress as though it was somehow to blame for her carelessness.

She thought to make an apology but for a reason unbeknown she said, "If I wanted to show my appreciation I would find a more pleasurable way of doing so."

Tristan raised a brow as he folded his arms across his broad chest. "Now you have my full attention. What sort of thing did you have in mind?"

Exchanging flirtatious quips with him had always proved entertaining. "Well, with these nimble fingers," she said, holding her hand up and wiggling the digits, "I could entertain you for hours."

He cleared his throat and moistened his lips. "What a delightful thought."

"Of course, I shall need to dust off the pianoforte as it has not been played in years."

The smile touching the corners of his mouth caused a shiver of awareness to race through her.

"I have always found music soothes my soul," he said in a rich tone. "Indeed, I am confident that once you find your rhythm, I shall be thoroughly entertained."

A snigger burst from her lips. It felt wonderful to laugh again.

His eyes sparkled like the sun's reflection on water. When he laughed she knew it to be genuine for his smile illuminated his face. In that moment, he was just as she remembered. The faint creases around his mouth, and the bronzed tint to his skin proved to be the only evidence that any time had passed.

"Do you remember the day you chased me around the fountain, and you slipped and fell in?" She chuckled again at the memory. His coat had clung to his muscular arms; his boots squelched when he walked. "I laughed until it hurt. An hour passed before I could breathe properly again."

He nodded. "I remember. I wanted to scoop you up in my arms until you were soaked through, too."

"You did? Why ... why didn't you?"

He contemplated her question. "I suppose I wanted you to think me a gentleman."

His answer surprised her. She'd always thought him respectful, considerate. That was until he abandoned her. Even now, that decision still seemed so completely out of character.

"Well, only a gentleman would give up his time to save a damsel in distress," she said, choosing to show her gratitude for his intervention instead of dwelling on the past. "Only a gentleman would listen to stories of ghosts and phantoms without declaring me insane."

His arms fell to his side as he straightened. "We will find a plausible explanation for the strange events here."

"Then let us begin our investigation this instant." She turned, closed her chamber door and gestured for him to follow her along the landing. "I thought it best to start with a tour of the house unless you have other ideas."

"I have spoken to Jacob. He informed me that a Mr. Blackwood is employed to manage the estate. With your permission, I would like to speak to him." He stopped and turned to face her. "If I am to help you, I need you to tell me everything," he whispered.

Isabella swallowed. "Everything?"

"Everything involving your personal situation." He coughed into his clenched fist. "If I am to attempt to discover a motive for murder, then I must know what financial arrangements were made for you upon your husband's death."

"A motive for murder," she repeated. He sounded so confident in his ability to succeed. It brought to mind an earlier comment. He had not spent his time in France in pursuit of pleasure, but in catching criminals.

"You will need to be completely honest with me," he said,

averting his gaze to glance at the floor. "There can be no secrets between us."

Being honest with him had never posed a problem for her. "What do you want to know?"

He paused, swallowed audibly. "The nature of your relationship with your husband. Details of his relationship with his son. Who owns Highley Grange? Why it is Henry Fernall maintains control? Can you trust the staff here?"

"Goodness." She placed her hand to her chest. "Why did you not just say you wanted to know every intimate detail of my life? I am surprised you've not asked if I have a lover."

The comment was made in jest, purely to express her shock at the depth of information required.

His expression darkened. "Do you have a lover, Isabella?" His penetrating stare made her shift uncomfortably. "Your husband has been dead these last two years. It would be a natural assumption for anyone to make."

She had only ever had one lover. There had only ever been one man who made her body ache at the thought of joining with him. Of course, she had given herself to her husband on numerous occasions. But that was not love. It amounted to nothing more than one's duty.

Straightening her spine, she decided it was best to be blunt. "You are the only man I would class as such. A lover is someone who rouses an ardent passion, someone with whom you share a deep emotional connection." She flicked her hair in an act of disgruntlement. "So no, Tristan. Whilst I did my duty by my husband, other than you, there has been no one else."

He pushed his hand through his slightly damp locks, rubbed back and forth as though the motion would ease the tense expression on his face. "What … what happened between us … you must know that it meant something to me."

"Did it?" Her tone carried a hint of reproof. He wanted

honesty, and she would give it to him. "How would I know that?"

Pain flashed briefly in his eyes. "We were in love. It was inevitable we would find a way to express all we felt, all we meant to one another."

Did he not know that his words cut her to the bone? To remind her of what she had lost was akin to torture.

Thankfully, Mrs. Birch appeared at the top of the stairs. She cleared her throat and offered a curtsy. "I've prepared a light repast, my lady, a broth to warm up your bones. It's always wise to have a hot meal when caught out in weather such as this."

Isabella forced a smile. It took a moment for her to focus on forming a response. While her body was in the present, her mind lingered in the past. "Yes. Thank you, Mrs. Birch. We will be right down."

Mrs. Birch nodded and made a hasty retreat.

"Come. Let us go and eat." He waved his hand for her to lead the way. "We can continue our discussion downstairs, though there are certain questions you should not answer unless we can ensure absolute privacy."

He sounded serious, so sober. She preferred his tone playful, teasing, brimming with amusement. Though they remained silent as they made their way to the dining room, she sensed a heavy pressure in the air that suggested he was deep in thought.

They chose to sit at the far end of the table, in the seats closest to the fire. Other than passing pleasantries (a mutual admiration for the landscape painting that hung above the fireplace, their predictions of how long it would be before the rain stopped) they ate their meal in silence. She watched him from beneath hooded lids, noted the lock of golden hair that fell to cover his brow, averted her gaze whenever he looked up.

"You said you wanted to know who owns Highley Grange." She could not continue to stare at him without saying something. "What made you think that I do not?"

He used his napkin to dab at the corners of his mouth. "It is something Jacob said."

"Jacob? What ... what did he say?"

"I spoke to him briefly when I rode round to the stable. As I said, he mentioned that Mr. Blackwood manages the estate. That it is Henry Fernall who pays the servants' wages." He paused. "How do you find Mr. Blackwood?"

"Mr. Blackwood?" She rarely saw the man. "He is hardly ever about when I am in residence."

During the rare occasions when their paths did happen to cross, he struggled to hold her gaze. Not that she was complaining. His thick eyebrows gave his face a wild, almost feral appearance that made the hairs at her nape stand on end.

"Does that not strike you as odd? Surely there are matters of estate business that require some communication."

She shrugged. "Henry keeps him busy."

"As the heir, it is reasonable to expect Henry to oversee things. But something tells me his interest in Highley Grange stems from more than a need to be helpful."

"Henry owns Highley Grange." And oh, how he enjoyed reminding her of the fact. "He is responsible for everything. As per the stipulations of my husband's will, I am permitted to live here until I remarry or until I meet my demise."

Tristan's eyes widened. "Why did you not mention it before? Perhaps Henry wants rid of you. It gives him motive."

"Perhaps it gives him a motive to frighten me but not to murder his own father."

"Shush. Keep your voice low." Tristan glanced at the open door. "I assume you have been provided for financially."

"I have a small allowance." She was not frivolous, and so it was adequate for her tastes. "I'm told circumstances would have been different if I'd had a child."

He sat back and closed his eyes briefly. "Has there ever been a child?"

It took a moment for her to comprehend his meaning. "No. Thankfully, I have never had to deal with such a terrible loss." Still, she felt the dull ache in her chest at the thought of never being a mother.

"But you were married for three years."

The snigger of contempt was louder than she anticipated. "It takes a little more than marriage to produce a child."

"I know that. Are you telling me you rarely ..." He waved his hand as a means of conveying the word he struggled to say.

"Yes. *Rarely* is the appropriate term."

He searched her face, his gaze falling to her neck, slightly lower. "Was Lord Fernall blind or simply stupid?"

The indirect compliment caused a warm glow to flow through her. It felt as though someone had wrapped her cold and aching limbs in a blanket of soft, fluffy down. Though she tried to suppress it, the corners of her mouth curled into a smile.

"We were unsuited. I suppose he hoped that taking a younger bride would solve the little problem he had." Samuel Fernall's preferences in the bedchamber beggared belief. "Well, I speak of the problem he had when trying to perform under normal circumstances."

Tristan's quizzical stare turned menacing. "Please tell me he did not hurt you."

Various images forced their way into her mind: the times Samuel begged her to pleasure herself whilst he watched from the shadows. His puffy red face swollen in anger as the insults burst cruelly from his lips. Like an annoying fly, she could not quite bat the visions away. Had her heart been whole, had her confidence not been left in tatters, Samuel would have hurt her terribly.

"I was immune to his cutting remarks. I was immune to the humiliation any wife would have felt upon discovering her husband kept a house purely for his sordid little parties."

Tristan glanced around the room. The frown marring his

brow convinced her that he was perhaps more perceptive than she thought.

"Am I correct to assume you speak of this house?"

She swallowed another spoonful of broth and nodded. "I suspect he meant to torment me for his many failings. It is strange how men blame their own inadequacies on their wives. In forcing me to live here, he is still able to punish me even from beyond the grave."

A tense silence filled the room.

After what felt like an eternity, Tristan stood abruptly. "Come. I believe the rain has stopped," he said, glancing out of the window. "Let us take a walk as we are both in need of some air."

"That is an excellent idea. There is something about this house I find quite suffocating." She forced a smile. She needed a little light relief after the pressure of such heavy scrutiny. "I will give you a tour of the gardens. It will do us good to stretch our legs. And now we have warmed our bones I doubt we will be in danger of catching a chill."

His curious gaze scanned her plain grey dress. "I will wait while you fetch your jacket."

"I shall be fine in this," she said, tugging at her sleeve. "The material is far too thick for this time of year."

She noticed his raised brow and knew another question was about to fall from his lips.

"I cannot help but notice you seem to prefer dressing in black or grey. The mourning period for your husband passed long ago. Does your subdued attire stem out of respect for Andrew?"

The question came as no surprise. He knew she once favoured bright colours: yellow ribbon on her bonnet, bright pink rosebuds embroidered on her shawl. She often made him wait while she picked vibrant flowers to fill the vase in her bedchamber.

"I do miss Andrew, but no. Over the years I suppose I grew accustomed to the drab colours." She did not want him to know that, since their separation, she could not bear anything that reminded her of their time together. "And it is so easy to coordinate on a budget," she added with a hint of amusement as he followed her into the drawing room and out through the doors leading to a small terrace.

He smiled at her last comment. "When we have found a plausible explanation for the strange happenings in the house, perhaps you should accompany me on a shopping expedition. We shall find material for a dress, something bold, something striking in a hue of rich golden yellow."

It took every ounce of strength she had to hold the tears at bay. A year after Tristan had left, and in an act of defiance, she'd had a gown made in daffodil yellow. Although try as she might, she could not wear it. "I would like that," she said, though her throat felt tight and it proved difficult to swallow.

They spent a few hours strolling in the garden. The sun made an appearance, the brilliant rays working to soothe away any tension. As they meandered through the avenues of sculptured topiary, he told her of the changes he wanted to make to the gardens at Kempston Hall.

"During my time at the monastery, I often spent time in the garth. With walls on every side, it forces you to stare up at the sky. The longer I sat there, the more my soul felt lighter, free."

"So you would not plant shrubs?"

"No. I would do nothing to distract the eye."

She led him to the walled garden, agreed that the roses did indeed draw one's attention away from the vast blue canopy above. He persuaded her to pick the flowers from the beds to be arranged in a crystal vase and placed in her room. They laughed over silly things, walked in companionable silence.

It was as though they had never been apart.

After dinner, they sat in the drawing room. He spoke of his

wild escapades in France. Imagining him in his French lover's arms had kept her awake at night many times over the years. Indeed, the thought plagued her even now.

"What should I do if I hear or see anything strange tonight?" she asked as they climbed the stairs. Being in his company made her forget all about her woes. It wasn't until he suggested they retire early that the morbid thoughts returned.

"If you're able, knock on my door. Call out if you fear leaving your bed." He opened the door of her chamber and stepped aside for her to enter. "Would you like me to check your room?"

Panic flared. Her heart thumped wildly in her chest at the thought of being alone with him in her private chamber. Just a few days ago, she had sat across from him in her carriage believing herself lacking when it came to feeling any genuine emotion. Now, desire blossomed, unfurling slowly like the petals of a spring bud.

"No. I'm confident it will be fine. And you will be just across the hall."

He raised his chin in acknowledgement. "I suppose I should wish you a peaceful night, but it would help our cause if something unusual did happen."

She hugged the edge of the door, watched him as he walked across the landing to open his door. "I'm sure it will be a long night. I doubt either of us will sleep."

Stepping inside his room, he turned to face her. "After all my probing questions, you're bound to be in need of a little rest."

It was her cue to yawn and bid him goodnight, but something kept her there.

"My head *is* throbbing from your relentless prying," she said with a chuckle. "Perhaps it is only fair I get to ask a question of my own before we retire."

The corners of his mouth twitched. "We did agree to be honest. You may ask whatever you wish."

*Why did you not want me?*

*What did I do to make you stop loving me?*

The questions did not suddenly spring into her mind. She carried them around with her always. A permanent reminder of her inadequacy. But she would not demean herself by demanding an answer.

"You asked me something extremely personal, something intimate. I would like you to answer the same question." She stood rigid, hoping her taut muscles would shield her from the blow she knew was coming. "Do *you* have a lover? Is that why you do not appear enamoured with Miss Smythe?"

Tristan stared at her; his expression wavered. One moment she saw a glint of pleasure in his bright blue eyes, the next she saw sadness and pain. A heavy tension hung in the air.

"No. I do not have a lover."

Despite his melancholic tone, relief coursed through her. Why should she feel so elated? Why did she want to clap her hands, sing and jump for joy?

She scrambled about in her mind, trying to find the right words to reflect her surprise without revealing anything more. But Tristan took a step back.

"I do not have a lover," he repeated as he closed the door slowly. "There has never been anyone other than you."

# CHAPTER 8

*T*ristan pressed his back against the bedchamber door and closed his eyes.

*Bloody hell!*

He exhaled deeply. The long weary sound drifted through the room until all the air had left his lungs.

Of all the things he could have said, the declaration proved that he had not been able to move forward with his life. Revealing his secret roused an uncomfortable sense of vulnerability that did not sit well with him. Muttered curses continued to fall from his lips.

Whilst perhaps appearing rude, his sudden retreat was merely a defensive manoeuvre.

Should he open the door and offer an explanation? Should he demand she put him out of his misery, tell him what he had done to force her into the arms of another man?

Pushing away from the door, he raked his hand through his hair. One thing was certain. He could not go on pretending the past didn't matter. Although bitterness lingered deep within, he still wanted her. More than ever.

God, he was a damn fool.

Perhaps Chandler was right. A discreet liaison would serve his purpose. Burying himself inside Isabella's tempting body would help him to banish the demons of the past. But she had rejected him once before. Why would she want him now?

Feeling a desperate urge to find a distraction from his conflicting thoughts, he scanned the dimly lit room. From the drapes to the bed hangings, the various shades of blue created a cold, detached feeling, one so opposed to the fiery heat coursing through his veins when he thought of the tempting lady just across the hall.

So this was the room Lord Fernall slept in before he died.

Isabella had given him the option of choosing a different bedchamber, but logic dictated that he remain close. Besides, his time in France had seen him sleeping in barns, stables, a blanket laid out on the forest floor. And so he was grateful to have a bed. Sentiment played no part in his decision.

Stripping down to his breeches and shirt, he climbed onto the bed and lay back against the mound of pillows. He crossed his arms behind his head and surveyed the room. Nothing captured his attention. Everything was exactly as one would expect. There was a washstand, his shaving implements laid out in an orderly fashion on top of the marble surface, an armoire which he assumed now contained the spare shirt and breeches he had brought with him in a saddle bag. The tall bookcase opposite the bed was crammed with a collection of dusty old tomes.

Well, at least if he struggled to sleep he would have something to read.

Reaching for his pocket watch, which he had placed on the side table next to the bed, he noted it was only eleven o'clock. Most ghosts and spectres chose to wait until after midnight before performing their devilish tricks. There was something about the early hours that created a perfect setting for a haunting. Perhaps it had something to do with the depressingly dark atmosphere or the eerie sound of silence.

Knowing sleep would elude him, he closed his eyes and attempted to clear his mind.

An hour passed.

The distant chimes of the clock in the hallway downstairs indicated the witching hour was upon them.

There was a chance his presence would prevent the perpetrator from acting. Then again, fear was contagious. Having a witness to corroborate the terrifying events would only help to strengthen their cause.

While he tried to piece together what little he knew, he found his thoughts wandering back and forth. Whimsical dreams of Isabella pushed to the fore. Lost in the warm, pleasurable feeling such visions evoked, he must have missed the single chime to indicate it was one o'clock.

However, it was not the chimes for two that captured his attention. The sound of approaching footsteps forced him to sit up. Sliding quietly off the bed, he crept to the door, pressed his ear against it and tried to distinguish any obvious characteristics.

The steps were not the heavy tread of masculine feet, but more a light patter. The short strides indicated a woman of small stature. They stopped outside his door. The hard lump in Tristan's throat made it difficult for him to swallow. His blood rushed through his veins. Only a fool would open the door.

Turning the handle slowly, he used his other hand to ease the door away from the jamb. Whilst he knew damn well he would not find a ghost on the other side, he did not wish to alert the person of his intention.

But there was no one lurking outside his door.

Gripping the frame, he peered out along the hallway. It was empty, too. Feeling some confusion, he padded down the long corridor. No one lurked in the shadows. There was no sign of a figure moving furtively down the stairs.

He turned and opened the first door to his left, glanced inside but found nothing. As he made his way back to his room, he heard Isabella's desperate plea.

"Please, stop. Go away. Leave me alone."

Panic flared.

Tristan raced to her door and tapped twice. "Isabella," he whispered. "Isabella."

"No, don't."

Without giving the matter another thought, he charged into her chamber.

The dancing flame in the candle lamp on the dressing table cast a faint golden hue over the room. He scanned the shadows for any sign of an intruder. Again the room was empty. The thick red drapes on the large four-poster bed were drawn. He feared someone was hiding inside.

"Don't," Isabella cried.

Tristan dragged back the bed hangings to find no one other than an ebony-haired temptress stretched out on the bed. Every soft curve was visible through the thin white nightdress as she writhed back and forth, lost in a distressing dream. He pinched his arm, fearing he was dreaming, too.

With trembling fingers, he touched her hand. "Isabella. Wake up. Can you hear me?"

She woke with a start, sat bolt upright, her eyes wide, fearful. "What?" She sucked in a breath, blinked numerous times. "Tristan?"

"You were dreaming," he said softly as he sat on the edge of the bed.

"Tristan!" With a sigh of relief, she wrapped her arms around his neck and hugged him tight. "My dream ... it was so real. I thought I was alone."

Dismissing his shock at the affectionate gesture, he ran his palm over her back in soothing, circular strokes, fought the selfish urge to capture her mouth and make her forget all the imagined horrors. "I heard you call out. I would not have entered your chamber had I not thought you were in distress."

He chose not to tell her about the footsteps along the hall. Being a man of sound rational mind, he knew he would find a logical explanation.

Isabella moved to lay her head on his shoulder. "I'm so glad you're with me. I would rather join the nuns at St. Augustus than stay here on my own."

Her whispered words breezed across the sensitive skin on his neck. A pleasurable shiver raced through him. Knowing that he had to place some distance between them for fear of losing his mind to the lustful pangs that racked his body, he eased her arms from around his neck and forced her to straighten.

"I'll not leave here until we have caught the culprit."

She sucked in a whimper. "Do you promise?"

The desperation in her voice touched his heart. He cupped her face with both hands. "I promise."

They stared at each other for the longest time. Her rich brown eyes searched his face. Many times he had lost himself in their dark, unfathomable depths. His gaze dropped to the luscious lips moving closer in mute invitation.

Just one brush would suffice. Just one sweet, chaste kiss.

The temptation proved too great.

He bent his head, eager to taste the only woman he had ever wanted. The erratic beat of his heart hammered in his ears. With his mouth hovering a mere inch above hers, he hesitated. They were so close their breath mingled in the space between them. When she pressed her open mouth to his, he closed his eyes, seared the sensation to memory.

The kiss was slow, tender, the pressure light. Still, the touch of her lips rocked him to his core. It was not a lustful claiming. It was more a soothing caress, a sensual massage for the soul.

She pulled away, just a fraction, yet he could feel her breath breeze across his lips. Disappointment became a sinking feeling of despair. But as his mind scrambled to decide what to do, her mouth recaptured his with a level of raw hunger that belied any outward calm.

Their hesitant tongues touched. The sound of her ragged breathing was music to his ears. He crushed her to his chest, drank deeply, their tongues thrusting wildly in a dance that made every part of him swell. Her frantic fingers found their way into his hair. He pulled her closer, desperate for the heat of her body to warm his cold, lonely heart.

Sweet Jesus. The tips of her nipples brushed against the fine lawn of his shirt, and he knew he would not be able to stop until he had sated five years' worth of lust and longing.

The sudden tapping noise coming from his room across the hall caused them both to jump back. He forced his gaze away from Isabella's swollen lips, torn between pulling her back into his arms and going to investigate the suspicious sound.

"Did you hear that?" Isabella clutched his arm. "There is someone in your room."

He covered her hand with his own. "We would have heard him coming up the stairs," he said to reassure her, although there was every possibility that the footsteps he'd heard earlier were made by the same person. "Wait here. I shall be back in a moment."

"No. I'm coming, too. You cannot leave me here alone."

It was a reasonable request. "Very well." He stood, shuffled uncomfortably to ease the throbbing ache filling his breeches and held out his hand to her. "You must stay behind me but stay close."

Her dainty palm settled against his. The pleasurable sensation that accompanied the intimate gesture served to bolster his courage. They crept out into the hall, entered his chamber with a level of extreme wariness.

Once again the room was empty, dark.

It did not make any sense. He had left the candle flickering in its metal holder. Glancing at the side table, he noticed an adequate enough stub to last for another hour, maybe more. Perhaps a sudden draft had blown it out.

With a firm grip of her hand, he moved over to the window and pulled back the drapes. "Perhaps a bird flew into the glass," he said, trying to think of any reason to account for the odd noise, other than the possibility that it was made by a ghost.

"As a man who is usually so logical, I know you don't believe that." Isabella screwed up her nose. "There are no birds about at this hour of the morning. Besides, it sounded like someone tapping on wood."

Tristan turned back in an attempt to look for the source. He sucked in a breath, unprepared for the sight that greeted him.

Isabella gasped. "I told you," she cried as they stared at the writing on the wall adjacent to the door. "Now will you believe me when I tell you there is no explanation for the strange things that go on here?"

Against the blue flock wallpaper the words *get out* were scrawled in some sort of luminous substance. In the dark, the command had the appearance of an ominous warning from beyond the grave.

Tristan stepped closer, keen to observe the markings. He came to an abrupt halt but a foot or so away. Isabella stood at his side as they stared at the words for a moment. The faint odour lingering in the air confirmed his suspicions.

"Don't touch it," he said, lightly tapping her outstretched fingers as one would do to a curious child. "If I am correct, it is white phosphorous and can cause severe burns if it comes into contact with the skin."

She dropped her hand. "How did it get there?"

Tristan glanced back over his shoulder. Nothing appeared out of place. Other than the extinguished candle, the room was exactly as he had left it mere moments before.

"I have no notion, but one thing is clear. A ghost—"

He stopped abruptly. The torturous groan emanating from Isabella's room was accompanied by a range of strange tapping noises. Tristan held on to her hand as he pulled her across the landing.

"Whoever it is, they have us scurrying about like blasted mice." His words revealed frustration rather than fear. They entered her chamber, were greeted by an eerie silence. "If only we knew where the sound was coming from," he whispered.

"Perhaps we should call out." She straightened her spine yet kept a firm grip of his hand. "Tap once if you want me to leave this house." Isabella's sudden request shocked him.

"There are no ghosts—"

"Shush. Just listen."

The single tap rang through the room, loud and clear.

Tristan attempted to locate the sound. It definitely came from the right-hand side of the room. "Ask something else."

She nodded. "Tap twice if you are the spirit of Lady Mary Fernall."

The double tap came from the room across the hall. Tristan had no idea how the person responsible was capable of being in two places at once, but he would not rest until he discovered the answer.

"Do not say any more," he said, taking her hand and backing out of the room.

They were a few steps from the door when the outline of a figure caught his eye. "Wait. There is someone over there on the bed."

At first glance, it appeared as though the person was sleeping. Locks of ebony hair lay sprawled over the pillow. The body was shrouded by the coverlet.

"Stay behind me," he said as they approached with caution. With his clenched fist raised ready to hit out, he dragged the red and gold cover off the bed.

Isabella's scream rang in his ears. She clutched his shirt. "What is it?"

Tristan stared at the grey dress draped over a line of pillows. "It is nothing more than another attempt to frighten you."

Stepping closer he picked up the black wig. "Does this belong to you?" he said, throwing it back on the bed.

She came to his side. "I have never seen it before. But that is my dress."

As he moved the dress, he noted the large red circular stain.

"Is it ... is it blood?" she stuttered.

Tristan lifted it to his nose, wet his finger and dabbed at the mark. "No. If I am not mistaken, it is wine."

"Wine?"

"Blood is lighter in colour, the consistency much thicker, even on fabric."

"You sound as though you speak from experience."

"In bouts of drunkenness I have spilt more than my fair share of wine," he said in an attempt to lighten the mood. "Come. This proves we are not dealing with a spiritual entity. Our best option is to ignore it. Help me tidy the bed. And then you should get some rest. We have a busy day ahead of us tomorrow."

Her wild gaze darted about the room. "I cannot sleep after all that has occurred."

Tristan turned to face her fully. He stepped closer and whispered, "Everything we have seen and heard has been a series of incidents conducted with the intention of frightening you from your home. Perhaps the person responsible thinks me just another pompous lord, too preoccupied with the frivolities of life and lacking the ability of good sense and reason. But they have made a dreadful miscalculation."

Isabella put her hand to her heart. "I do not know what I would have done had you not been here."

He touched his finger to her sumptuous lips. "We must be careful what we say whilst in this room." Jerking his head, he gestured to the door. "Let us vacate this chamber and find one further along the hall."

Isabella nodded. Taking the candle lamp from the dressing table, they moved to the room nearest the stairs. With its white and gilt furniture and vivid yellow walls, the chamber was brighter, far more fashionable, although the bed was only large enough for one.

"This should suffice," he said, forcing a smile to hide his frustration. As soon as he'd heard the sounds and found the message painted on the wall, he should have bolted down to the servants' quarters and checked they were all in their beds. It was too late now. Distracted by the pile of pillows and wine-stained dress, they had given the culprit ample time to flee.

Isabella pulled back the sheets and sat on the edge of the bed. "You said we have much to do tomorrow. Does that mean you have a plan?"

"We will conduct a thorough search of the rooms. Speak to the servants. I want to visit the gatehouse, to ensure Mr. Black-wood is not at home. You must also tell me as much as you can about your relationship with Andrew."

She sighed as she climbed into bed and placed her head on the pillow. "I suspect such a thorough investigation will take us all day." There was a nervous hitch in her voice. "And then I suppose you must leave. You are far too busy to spend your time here."

The sadness in her eyes belied her casual tone.

Tristan came to stand next to the bed. "I'll not leave you." He bent down and brushed a lock of ebony hair from her face. "Try to get some sleep. I shall spend the next few hours over there in the chair."

She nibbled on her bottom lip. "But it will be uncomfortable."

"Trust me. I have slept in worse places." It would be far more uncomfortable lying next to her when all he wanted to do

83

was take her in his arms and banish the ghosts for good. "Besides, the bed is too small for two."

An image of him covering her body flashed into his mind, purely to prove there were other positions available should they wish to share a bed.

Tristan walked over to the door and turned the key in the lock.

"Why are you locking the door? I thought you did not believe in ghosts."

He smiled. "I don't. It is the living we must protect ourselves from."

## CHAPTER 9

*J*sabella opened her eyes and stretched her arms above her head. Finding her surroundings somewhat unfamiliar, it took a moment to recall the reason for moving to another chamber. She propped herself up on her elbows and scanned the room.

Whilst the yellow drapes served to prevent the morning sun streaming in, by the very nature of their vibrancy they cast a golden glow over the gentleman sleeping in the chair. With his cheek resting in the palm of his hand, and a lock of fair hair falling over his brow, he appeared peaceful, angelic.

A soft sigh left her lips.

She watched the gentle rise and fall of his chest with some fascination. He might look pure and saintly, but there was nothing innocent about the way he'd kissed her. His wicked mouth had claimed hers with a level of unbridled passion that was positively sinful. She touched the tips of her fingers to her lips as she recalled the heavenly memory.

It had been a mad moment of weakness. It had been a desperate urge to relive a happy moment from her past. Yet she knew that succumbing to her desire for a man who refused to commit would only lead to more pain. Despite it all, kissing Tristan did not feel wrong. In Tristan's company she felt safe; in his arms she felt complete.

*There has never been anyone other than you.*

His words echoed through her mind once more, just to torment her. What did he mean? In the five years since their separation, he must have taken another woman to his bed. The depth of passion emanating from him during their salacious kiss proved his penchant for carnal pleasures. Perhaps he thought that to declare himself celibate would help to heal the wounds of rejection. Perhaps he simply meant that, since breaking his promise to her, he had not proclaimed love to anyone else.

It was all rather baffling.

Just as baffling as the eerie events they had witnessed a few hours earlier. Had she been alone in a cold, dark chamber, she might have expired from the shock. Then again, without Tristan's assistance, she would not have found the courage to return to Highley Grange.

"Why did you not wake me?" Tristan's sleepy drawl caused her heart to miss a beat. He sat up straight, yawned then rubbed the muscles in his neck. "I think it would have been more comfortable to sleep on the floor."

Guilt flared. "I know it is probably not much consolation, but I do appreciate you being here."

His languid gaze drifted over her before settling on her hair. "I see you managed to sleep, although it appears to have been a somewhat restless affair. After all that occurred in the early hours, I doubted you would."

"It took a while," she said, patting down her locks. "The tedious journey from London, coupled with getting caught in the torrential rain, must have taken its toll." She chose not to divulge that she had lost herself in whimsical daydreams, where passionate kisses were a prelude to something far more satisfying.

"Let us hope the weather has improved." He stood, stretched his arms out in front of him before parting the drapes and peering through the window. "At least the sun is shining this morning."

The conversation felt somewhat strained. She wondered if the tension stemmed from the kiss they had shared. Did regret form the basis of his detached tone?

"We should return to our rooms and dress before the servants discover we shared the same chamber." Her confident tone belied the nervous flutter in her stomach.

He turned to face her. "Have you ever spoken to the servants about the strange things happening here?"

"Only briefly." As mistress of the house, it was not wise to draw attention to one's emotional weaknesses. "They often speak of seeing a lady dressed in a white shroud." A chill shivered through her, and she pulled the coverlet up over her shoulders. "Mrs. Birch believes it is Mary, the ghost of Samuel's first wife."

Tristan came and sat on the end of the bed. The intimate action conveyed a relaxed ease in her company, one so opposed to his dispassionate demeanour when discussing the strange events. Even so, she could not help but stare at his mouth.

"Has your housekeeper said what makes her think that?"

"No. But Mary Fernall never spent a single night in this house." Given the option, Isabella would not have done so, either. "I was always of the opinion that ghosts haunted familiar places."

"There are no ghosts here," Tristan reiterated with an amused snort. "Just a concerted effort to make you and others believe so."

She stared into his blue eyes, searching for reassurance. "I'm sure you are right."

"Trust me when I tell you I am determined to solve this mystery."

His confident manner served to enhance his appeal. In their youth, it had been his carefree attitude to life that had fed her attraction. His bright, cheerful countenance had helped to ease the pain of her mother's passing, forced her to seek out his company. Now, he was masterful without being overbearing. A raw and powerful masculine energy emanated from deep within. The overwhelming feeling of love and affection she still nurtured was now accompanied by a lustful yearning that sought to steal her breath.

She tried to swallow down her desire, suppressed the urge to say she needed him, needed him in every possible way. "What do you intend to do today?" she said, relieved to have asked a simple question without revealing the true nature of her inner thoughts.

"My priority will be to search both rooms at the end of the hall. I believe the answer to the mysterious haunting lies there."

A smile touched her lips. "When I asked for your help, I did not realise you would be so thorough, so systematic in your investigation. Without wishing to sound patronising, I'm impressed." It was a compliment, and she hoped he read it so.

"I do have experience when it comes to dissecting the criminal mind." The glint in his eye told her that he welcomed her praise.

"It is pleasing to know you put your time in France to good use."

His expression grew solemn. "Marcus Danbury taught me everything I know. He was more of a brother to me than Andrew ever was."

To discuss his relationship with his brother would only serve to aggravate his sudden mood. "It might comfort you to know that Andrew was aware of his failings. But there will be plenty of time for us to talk later." Indeed, an honest discussion about their past was long overdue. "But for now, we should focus on the task ahead."

With a curt nod, he stood. "Would you like me to find the maid and have her attend you in here?"

She gave a weak chuckle. "I am capable of dressing myself, Tristan. The house already runs on minimal staff. But thank you for thinking of me. I shall return to my room. I would rather not appear overly dramatic in front of the servants."

He inclined his head. "Then I shall be across the hall should you need me."

"Mrs. Birch wishes to convey her apologies for the lack of variety this morning." Isabella waved her hand over the silver serving dishes arranged neatly on the sideboard. "As I did not send word of our impending arrival she was rather unprepared." She chose not to tell him she had caught the servants playing cards and drinking her sherry.

Tristan filled his plate with bread rolls and various slices of cold meat. "This is more than ample. At the monastery, meals were far from extravagant."

They sat down on opposite sides of the table.

"You always speak of your time in France with such fondness." She found herself smiling as she spoke. Perhaps because the mere mention of his life abroad always brought a playful glint to his eye.

He sighed. "The people there became my family. Marcus is a good man. You would like him. There is nothing pretentious about his character." He chuckled to himself. "Although he can be incredibly stubborn most of the time."

Isabella felt a strange pang in her chest. As a young woman, she would have done anything to make Tristan happy. To acknowledge that she had played no part in the life that he regarded with such affection, hurt.

"Well, I for one am grateful you came back," she said, trying to banish the thought that he had chosen to leave her in order to find true happiness. "Your insight has been invaluable. Had it not been for you I would have touched the painted words smeared across the wall."

He swallowed whatever he had in his mouth. "It is often easier to assess a situation when you are not emotionally involved. Fear forces one to be less objective."

"Perhaps you're right. I hear a noise and think of ghosts. You hear a noise and understand that there must be a logical explanation. I shall be relieved to discover the answer."

He glanced down at the last slice of cold ham on his plate. "Give me five minutes and we shall go upstairs."

Her heart skipped a beat at the licentious implication of his words even though she knew what he meant. "I'm intrigued to know what we will find. I cannot imagine how someone was able to dress my bed so quickly only to disappear with no trace of ever having been there."

"Are you not eating?" he said, nodding to her plate. She glanced down, realised she had hardly touched a morsel. "Anxiety has a way of suppressing one's appetite."

A broken heart and pining for a lost love made one dissatisfied, too.

He stood and placed his napkin on the table. "Then let us get to it. Once we have discovered the truth, I am sure you'll be ravenous for dinner."

Tristan sat on the bed in Lord Fernall's room and stared at the words painted on the wallpaper. His initial observation had been correct. The luminous effect of the phosphorescent substance was diminished slightly by the daylight.

"But we would have seen or heard someone moving about in

here." Isabella glanced at him, her furrowed brow evidence of her confusion. "People do not just disappear."

"I agree," he said, rubbing his chin, "which means they found somewhere to hide during the process." He paused briefly while he considered the possibility. The gap between the wooden bed frame and the floor proved too small. A child would struggle to fit inside the armoire. "Let us go and inspect your room."

They walked across the hall and into her bedchamber.

"Perhaps they hid behind the drapes," she said as they stood in the middle of the room and scanned their surroundings. "Whoever dressed my bed had but a few minutes to do so."

"So, the aim is to frighten you into thinking the house is haunted, and that your life is in danger," Tristan reiterated more for his own benefit. He noted the bookcase on the wall opposite the bed. "Do you read often?"

She followed his gaze to the shelves of leather-bound books. "No. Everything you see is as it was when I took up residence. Whenever my funds permit it, I stay at the house in Brook Street."

Tristan struggled to suppress his irritated sigh. He did not approve of her flitting from one place to another. But in her refusal to marry him, she had denied him the right to pass comment.

"How long have you been experiencing the strange phenomena?"

Isabella tapped her lip as she gazed up at the ceiling. "Well, after Samuel's death I remained at Grangefields for a time. Samuel constantly accused me of being Henry's lover, so I was not surprised to discover he had made provisions for me to live alone here."

The muscles in Tristan's throat constricted, to the point he feared his words would sound more like a croak if he tried to speak. "Is … is there any basis for Samuel's fears?" He swallowed deeply. "After all, you are the same age as his son."

Isabella's expression darkened. "Of course not. Set aside the fact that I am his stepmother, and consequently, any affair would appear incestuous in my eyes, but I cannot abide him. I find him rude and overbearing. He has gone out of his way to belittle and undermine me at every opportunity."

Some men played the arrogant card when trying to entice a woman into their bed. "Hence the reason you rent a house when in London."

She nodded. "Precisely."

Perhaps Henry Fernall *was* smitten with his stepmother. Tristan's gaze drifted over her ebony locks tied in a simple knot. The grey dress was just as drab as the one she had worn the previous day, yet she had an inherent appeal that fuelled the fiery passion raging within. Henry Fernall could not have failed to notice her. Indeed, what better way was there to lure a woman into your arms than by making her believe her house is haunted?

"So did these strange events begin as soon as you moved to Highley Grange?" Tristan attempted to clarify.

"I spent the first year after Samuel's death either at Grangefields or the house in Brook Street. Since then, whenever I have stayed here something untoward has occurred. During the last few months, the incidents have become more frequent, more terrifying, though I have never experienced anything along the same scale or magnitude as we did last night."

Tristan suspected his presence had motivated the culprit to put on a better show. He walked over to the window seat, checked to ensure the top panel was secure and did not conceal a secret hiding place, before dropping onto the cushion.

"Was your h-husband a voracious reader?" Tristan asked.

"Not that I am aware." She glanced down at a nondescript point on the floor, twisted her foot back and forth in a ritual that revealed her slight embarrassment. "I doubt an interest in academia was at the forefront of his mind when he came here."

"Oh, and why would you think that?"

She swallowed audibly. "The house was used for private parties. The sort ladies never dare speak about." A weary sigh left her lips, the sound suggesting mental fatigue.

Isabella did not need to explain. Tristan knew men who spent many a night catering to their licentious tastes and lewd appetites.

"But you implied Lord Fernall had a problem in that regard," Tristan said. God, he hoped it was true. The thought of the old lord failing to join with Isabella was the only thing keeping him sane.

"He ... he did." She swallowed deeply again. "He took his pleasure from ... from watching others."

Tristan jumped to his feet. His heart thumped loudly, the sound echoing in his ears. "Please tell me he didn't make you perform—" Good God, he could not say the words.

"Heavens, no!" She waved her hands frantically in front of her. "I would rather die than suffer the humiliation. Besides, knowing I was his wife only served to exasperate his problem."

So Lord Fernall enjoyed watching his guests partake in amorous liaisons. Tristan wondered if his friends were aware of his depraved habit. Had one of them taken their revenge by pushing him down the stairs?

Tristan took to walking about the room as it helped him to think clearly. "Perhaps he was murdered by a disgruntled guest," he said, revealing his suspicions.

"To my knowledge, the people who came here were all of a like mind."

Good Lord. He glanced around the room, his mind concocting obscene images of portly, middle-aged gentlemen gathered around the bed. He shivered in disgust, raked both hands through his hair in a bid to erase the vision.

"So why have bookcases up here?" Tristan said in a mocking tone. "There is a perfectly decent library downstairs and by the sound of it no one had the slightest interest in reading once—"

Tristan stopped abruptly. He folded his arms across his chest and stared at the books lining the oak shelves.

Isabella came to stand at his side. "What is it?" She placed her hand on his forearm. Even through the fabric of his coat, he found the sensation soothing. "Your eyes are so wide you look as though you truly have seen a ghost."

"It never occurred to me before," he said, scrutinising the size and shape of the case. "But there are identical bookcases in both rooms at the end of this hall."

"What is so strange about that?" she said.

"I don't know of anyone who keeps this number of books in their bedchamber."

"Perhaps you have always been too preoccupied to notice." Her playful tone held no hint of spite or jealousy.

Isabella followed him as he moved to examine the books. The case consisted of five shelves, all containing books of a similar size. Even whilst standing directly in front of it, there was nothing unusual. He turned and glanced at the bed, turned back to observe the row of books at eye level.

"Help me remove all the books on this row." If his suspicion proved correct, they would only need to move the middle section. "Start with the ones in the centre."

They had removed four books when Isabella gasped. "What is that?" She took a step closer and peered into the gap. "It's a little window."

"It's a viewing screen." Everything was beginning to fall into place. "I'm certain there will be a similar window cut out of the bookcase in the master chamber."

With wide eyes, Isabella turned to him. "But … but that would mean there must be a space behind the wall. A space large enough for a man."

"Not just a space. I imagine there is a hidden room that runs along the entire length of this wall." He tapped the wall to the right of the case. The hollow sound confirmed his theory. "This has to be the way the ghost managed to move about without detection."

She raised a brow. "You do not need to say it in a way that makes me feel foolish. You must admit, we were both alarmed last night."

"*Confused* is the term I would use," he said offering a grin. "Now, stand back and I shall see if I can find the way into the room."

Using his shoulder and the weight of his body, Tristan attempted to move the bookcase. Remarkably, it did not even move an inch, nor did the books on the shelf slip or slide back and forth in the gap.

"Perhaps it is not a bookcase after all, but a door," Isabella suggested as she witnessed him struggle. "Perhaps there's a handle hidden somewhere."

It was the only logical answer.

Tristan removed all the books to the right of the case, only from those shelves at hand height, and placed them in a pile on the floor. One book proved to be nothing more than an empty casing used to conceal a brass knob.

"Here we are," he said, immense satisfaction evident in his tone. He turned the handle, resisted the urge to cheer as he eased the door from the jamb.

The long narrow room was sparsely furnished: a wash-stand, a few red damask chairs, a table with empty decanters, dusty glasses and partially burnt candles. There were no windows, no way for any natural light to filter through.

Tristan examined the other side of the fake bookcase. "Once in here, they only had to turn the handle to open the door. The hollow book casing meant we would not even notice anything unusual in the bedchamber." He pointed to the door at the far end of the room. "Using both doors they were able to move freely between rooms."

"But we were in our rooms last night. Surely we would have noticed someone coming in."

Guilt flared. "Before coming into your chamber, I heard footsteps padding along the hall. I left my room and ventured all the way down to the staircase." Like an unsuspecting fool, he had fallen for the simplest of traps. "Someone could have easily waited in one of the other rooms. They would have had ample opportunity to enter this concealed chamber through the door in my chamber."

Isabella gazed about the secret room. "How could I not know it was here? Surely the servants are aware." She visibly shivered. "Oh, and to think someone could have been watching me while I slept or bathed. I think I would rather it was a ghost."

Feeling a modicum of guilt for finding pleasure in the thought of watching her bathe, he shook the vision from his head.

She appeared forlorn, her expression one of hopelessness. Tristan stepped towards her, took hold of her chin and forced her to look at him. "Sometimes reality is far more gruesome than any imagined horrors. But only the truth can free you from your shackles. Take comfort in the knowledge that we are making progress, that we will uncover every dastardly plot so you may live in peace and comfort."

Isabella smiled weakly as she placed her hand over his. "Thank you, Tristan. Thank you for coming here to help me when I suspect it is the last thing you wanted to do."

Being with Isabella was the only thing he had ever wanted. "Our investigation is far from over. I am afraid you will have to tolerate me a little while longer."

"There is nothing sufferable about spending time with you," she said in a tone that made the hairs at his nape jump to attention. "I enjoy your company. I always have."

He felt the familiar pang in his chest, the familiar tug in his abdomen. Love and lust coursed through his veins. For the first time in years, he did not want to hear the truth from her lips. To be set free was the last thing he wanted. Being bound to her was all he lived for. He did not care what her reasons were for marrying Lord Fernall.

One way or another, he would find a way to make her his again.

# CHAPTER 10

*T*he atmosphere in the drawing room thrummed with palpable tension.

Isabella sat with her spine straight, her chin raised, her mouth stretched thin as she stared at her servants' solemn faces. They stood in a line, their hands held in front of them, their demeanour giving the impression they would be shot if they so much as blinked or breathed.

She glanced at Tristan standing in front of the fire with his hands clasped behind his back. His curt nod gave her the confidence to continue.

"Well, what have you to say?" When they failed to respond, she said, "Then I shall take your silence as an admission of guilt. As you have declined the opportunity to offer an explanation, you must all collect your things at once and leave this house immediately."

It was an idle threat. The servants were in Henry's employ. She could not simply dismiss them without consulting him first. Even so, Molly's whimper gave her a little faith that they were all close to confessing.

"It's not our fault, my lady," Molly cried. "What else were we to do?"

Mrs. Birch nudged the maid. "Since Lord Fernall's death, we have been warned not to mention the secret room. We were told not to remind you of the things that went on here."

"It is not the secret room that concerns me." One of the people in front of her had led a systematic campaign to frighten her out of her wits. "Which one of you covered my dress with wine and placed it in my bed? Which one of you sullied the wall with your cruel threats?" The sudden rush of anger forced her to her feet. "Which one of you sought to torment a lonely woman into believing her life was in danger?"

A sob caught in her throat and she swallowed it down.

Sedgewick bowed. "My lady, I am not to blame for these unfortunate events. My position in this household commands respect, and I would do nothing to hinder my position."

"What? Do your lofty manners prevent you from playing cards in the drawing room and drinking my sherry?" Isabella mocked.

Sedgewick's cheeks turned berry red. "A regrettable incident that will not happen again, my lady."

Isabella noted the piece of cloth tied around Molly's finger. "I am told the paint smeared over the wall in the master chamber burns when it comes into contact with the skin. Is that not correct, Lord Morford?"

"It is, Lady Fernall. Perhaps we should consider your maid's obvious injury to her finger as an admission of guilt."

"No, my lady," Molly cried, holding up the offending article. "I scalded it yesterday when heating the water for his lordship's bath." Her frantic gaze shot to Mrs. Birch. "Tell them it wasn't me who ruined the wallpaper. Tell them we had no choice but to do what Mr. Blackwood said."

"For goodness' sake, girl." Mrs. Birch shook her head and

with a grunt of resignation stepped forward. "Mr. Blackwood told us what we had to do."

Tristan straightened. "Did Mr. Blackwood say why you were to terrify your mistress?" The muscles in his cheek twitched. Anger radiated from him, hot and fiery. "Make no mistake. What you have done here could be regarded as deception, deception with the intent to cause harm."

The colour drained from their faces; their complexions turned ashen, their eyes wide with alarm.

"Causing my lady harm was never our intention." Mrs. Birch cleared her throat and turned her attention to Isabella. "Mr. Blackwood said Lord Fernall resents his father for forcing you to stay in this house. Lord Fernall thinks you should reside at Grangefields, a more respectable abode. This house is no place for a lady."

"Well, why did he not say so instead of devising such a ridiculous charade?"

"You'll have to ask his lordship. Mr. Blackwood is the one who passed on his instruction."

"And what of the hound I hear howling outside my window at night?"

Mrs. Birch lowered her gaze. "It's my nephew's dog. Mr. Blackwood trained him to sit in the same spot by burying fresh meat."

Isabella flopped down onto the gilt-framed settee. She was so tired. Since her mother's death she had struggled to settle, struggled to call any place her home. Her life during the last five years had been an awful lie. A marriage of convenience simply to ease her pain, to prove a point. A loveless arrangement to a gentleman known for his rakish behaviour and utter lack of morals.

Isabella stared at her housekeeper. "Was there a point in all of this where you questioned if what you were doing was wrong?"

Mrs. Birch nodded. "Mr. Blackwood can be very persuasive. He insisted it was for the best. We could see it was causing you distress which is the only reason we went to such great lengths last night."

Isabella could not even rouse the energy to pity them.

"You may all leave us," she said in a tone as cold as her heart. "Resume your duties until I tell you otherwise. I shall confer with Lord Fernall and decide what is to be done here."

The women offered a curtsy, Sedgewick a low bow, before retreating sombrely from the room.

Tristan came to sit beside her. "They were acting on instruction," he said. "I'm afraid their loyalty lies with the gentleman who employs them."

Isabella sighed; she was not so naive as to suppose it would be any different. "Perhaps they felt they were acting in everyone's best interest. But it reaffirms my need to find an alternative place to reside. I refuse to be beholden to Henry."

Tristan placed his hand over hers as they lay in her lap. "Do not be too hasty. We shall discuss the matter with Lord Fernall. Only then will you know how best to proceed."

She looked up into his piercing blue eyes. "We? You intend to accompany me when I call on Henry?"

"If that is what you want."

Emotions were a strange thing. Tristan had broken her heart, smashed it into a million tiny pieces. Now, every kind word and gesture went some way to help heal the damaged organ. Would it ever be whole again? Would she ever be capable of loving with the same passionate intensity?

"I do not know what to do." She glanced down at the large masculine hand enveloping hers. His warm touch made her pulse race a little too rapidly; it also brought a measure of peace, serenity. "Perhaps it is best not to think about it too much. They say a calm mind is a path to wisdom."

Tristan stood, walked over to the window and stared at the view beyond. "I suggest we stay here for the time being."

Her heart fluttered up to her throat. "Stay here?"

"I am certainly in no rush to return to London. Give yourself another day or two before you call on Henry Fernall."

He had promised to help her, and he had, but whilst they had solved the mystery of the haunting there was still the matter of murder to consider.

"The hauntings turned out to be nothing more than the work of an overbearing peer, but I am still convinced a murderer is lurking in our midst."

He turned to face her. "One thing is clear. The feigned hauntings bear no relation to Lord Fernall's death, or to Andrew's death for that matter. Perhaps they were both accidents. Perhaps fear played havoc with your imagination."

Isabella shook her head and clenched her jaw with a level of determination she rarely expressed. "You're wrong. Andrew believed me. He made enquiries, spoke to a few gentlemen who knew Samuel well. He kept a notebook—"

"I'm certain Andrew would have said or done anything just to spend more time in your company." His bitter tone sliced through the air. "Andrew always had an ulterior motive for everything he did."

She came to her feet and closed the gap between them. "Why can you not accept that he had changed? Do not mistake me. I found it so hard to forgive him for dragging me away from you that night at the coaching inn."

The mere mention of the night they eloped roused a host of painful memories. With the assistance of his coachman, Lord Morford had held Tristan at bay whilst Andrew had picked her up and bundled her into his carriage. She had cried until there were no tears left to shed. She had sworn never to forgive them for their treachery.

But loneliness and despair had overshadowed all other emotions.

"I will never forgive him." Tristan's expression darkened, and he narrowed his gaze. "But you do not need to pretend anymore. Andrew was your saviour, and that is why you were able to bear his company when I could not stand to look at him."

"My saviour?" She struggled to understand his meaning. "Yes, he helped me when Samuel died, when I had no one to turn to for guidance and support. In doing so, I forgave him for informing your mother of our elopement. I forgave him for ruining my life."

Tristan rubbed his neck as he gave a contemptuous snort. "I cannot believe I am about to defend my brother, but you are the only person responsible for ruining your life. Andrew did not force you to marry Lord Fernall."

Isabella swallowed down the hard lump in her throat. She clenched her fists for fear of slapping him. "No, Andrew did not force me into the arms of another man. You did, with your cold words and blatant disregard."

Tristan stared at her blankly. "I recall the last words spoken between us were at the coaching inn. I called out, told you I loved you. I told you no one would ever keep us apart."

Hearing the words fall from his lips brought the pain of the last five years flooding back. "But you said your affections for me stemmed from your need to defy your parents. You were reckless and thrived on the thrill that came with disobeying their wishes."

His mouth hung open; his frown created two deep furrows between his brows. "I never said that. Why would I say such a thing when it is not true?"

Her mind raced. Her chest grew tight, her face hot. "You said so in your letter."

"What letter?"

She struggled to breathe. "The letter you wrote to me on the night your father brought us both back to Kempston Hall."

"I am at a loss." He shook his head. "Why would I write to you when we prided ourselves on being so open and honest with one another?"

Panic flared. "Then be honest with me now."

"Trust me when I say I did not write to you."

She put her hand to the base of her throat. "But I have your letter here with me." She carried it around with her, had read it only the day before. She read it whenever she needed reminding that he did not want her. "It bears your signature."

There was a moment of silence.

The colour drained from his cheeks until his skin took on a deathly pallor. "Then I suggest you go and fetch this letter, Isabella, for I fear we have both been cruelly deceived."

# CHAPTER 11

*T*ristan paced back and forth while he waited for Isabella to return to the drawing room. He stopped, sat down on the settee, held his head in his hands as he attempted to make sense of their conversation.

One innocent comment, said in a fit of frustration, had now put everything he believed to be true into question. He rocked to ease the pressure building in his head. He could not bear to acknowledge the agonising ache wreaking havoc with his heart.

God, he hoped he was wrong. Living with the thought of her not wanting him had been torturous. To live knowing there had been a perfidious plan to keep them apart would be unbearable.

The door flew open. Isabella darted into the room in a state of agitation. "Here," she said, waving the heavily creased paper in the air. "This is the letter you sent to me."

Tristan jumped to his feet and closed the gap between them. With hesitant fingers, he took the letter from her hand. He was desperate to read it, yet he knew the words would bring nothing but pain.

He tried to assess the faded script logically: it was not written in his hand. The long, confident flourishes were the mark of an arrogant man. Sucking in a breath, he read the first line. There was nothing untoward. The tone conveyed a warmth of feeling: she meant the world to him, which was why he had no option but to let her go.

*My father was right. We are like kin. The love I feel is not what a man should feel for his wife. I made a mistake.*

"Hell and damnation!" He covered his mouth with his hand for fear of bringing Satan's curse down on everyone.

Isabella shuffled closer. Her flustered demeanour revealed an impatience for answers. "What is it, Tristan? Tell me. Now do you remember writing it?"

*It is best that you leave here, that you leave Kempston Hall, for to be together will only serve to bring us both unnecessary pain.*

Tristan tried to swallow, but his jaw held firm, locked and frozen in so rigid a position he was in danger of cracking the bone. Fury, red and hot, coursed through his veins. His vision grew hazy, the words on the paper lost in a blur.

"I did not write this." He wanted to shout as a way to release the pent-up emotion. But despair washed over him like a giant wave sweeping away all traces of anger. "I did not write this," he repeated quietly.

She grasped his arm. "What do you mean? Of course you wrote it." She blinked rapidly, her eyes overly bright. "You mentioned our walks in the garden. You spoke of our plans to wed."

Tristan shook his head. "I did not write it, Isabella."

"Then who—" She broke on a sob. Clutching her throat, she stared at him, confusion and fear giving way to anguish. "What are you saying? You ... you did not want me to leave Kempston? You did not want us to part?"

His throat was so tight he could barely speak. "I loved you. Why would I have wanted any of those things?"

Time stopped momentarily.

A heart-wrenching cry burst from Isabella's lips. "No! Please Lord, no." Her knees buckled; her legs gave way, and she crumpled to a heap on the floor. "Please, it cannot be true." She bowed her head, her body shaking as she sobbed uncontrollably.

In his dazed state, it took him a few seconds to react. He knelt down, put his hand on her shoulder. Damn, he could not stop the water welling in his eyes.

"Come," he said, knowing he had to remain calm for both their sakes. "Let me help you to your feet. Let us sit and talk."

Despite the painful emotions, vengeance flamed to life in his chest. Someone would pay. At this precise moment, he didn't care who.

He cupped her elbow, brought them both to their feet. She fell into his arms as her legs struggled to support her weight. For a time he held her there, rubbed his hand over her back in small circular motions until her breathing slowed.

"Tell me it is not true," she muttered into his chest. "I can live with loss but I cannot live with this." She pulled away and looked up at him, her puffy red eyes revealing the extent of her sorrow. "Do you know what hurts me most of all?"

"No." The word was quieter than a whisper.

"You went away believing I did not love you."

He sighed as he brushed a lock of ebony hair from her face. "I was told you had made a mistake. I woke to find you gone, soon discovered you had married."

She closed her eyes briefly as another tear fell. "And so ... so you ran away to France. You've spent five years believing I abandoned you to marry another. I can understand why you did not want to come home."

He would have done anything to avoid seeing her again. He should have had more faith. "Mr. Chandler told me that illogical behaviour often stems from a misunderstanding. I would have questioned your motives for leaving had I been given more time."

"Then I am the one to blame." She shook her head vigorously. "I should have come to you. I should have demanded an explanation before running off into the night. My only defence is that I was vulnerable, a young girl without family, a young girl so easily manipulated by those she thought she could trust."

"We are not to blame," he said firmly. The guilt was not theirs to bear. "Someone ruined our lives for their own purpose, and I will not rest until I discover the reason why."

She gave a weak smile. "Then know that I feel the same way. But all is not lost. We have salvaged something from the wreckage. You came to my aid when I needed help even though you were convinced I had abandoned you to marry another. That is the sign of a true friend, Tristan. Whatever wickedness was at play here, they have not succeeded in their effort to keep us apart. Despite all we believed to be true, we were able to put our differences aside and come together."

"And together we will find the answers. We will discover the truth." He glanced at the drinks tray, at the amber liquid calling to him from the decanter. "I'm in need of a drink, and then we shall sit down and relive the painful memories of that night."

"Then I shall join you," she said, dabbing the corner of her eye with the pad of her finger. "We must be honest with each other now, though I know it will hurt."

He poured himself a glass of brandy, her a sherry, remained silent through the process for his mind continued to recall the gut-wrenching moment his mother told him Isabella had married Lord Fernall.

"These things are for the best," his mother had said. "The girl obviously doesn't care for you."

Those words had been a lie.

Someone had written the letter on his behalf. While the motive for such an evil betrayal eluded him, there were but three people with the opportunity to deceive. His father and brother were dead. With only his mother left to question, he had to accept there was a possibility he would never discover the truth.

"I keep replaying the events over in my mind," Isabella said as he handed her the glass of sherry before sitting in the chair opposite. "I find myself forced to question Andrew's motives for being so kind to me these last few years. And I do not want to think ill of him when he is not here to defend himself."

"Based on what we know, it is fair to say that at least one member of my family was involved in the deception." He swallowed his brandy, let the warmth of the spirit soothe him. "Andrew was spoilt, often jealous. It would not surprise me to learn he acted out of spite. He was the only person who knew of our elopement. He expected us to leave Kempston in the dead of night, which was why I chose to hire a carriage and leave at noon."

"You meant to give us a few hours' start?"

"I knew he would not think to alert my parents until we failed to come down for dinner."

She smiled. "You never mentioned any of this at the time."

He inclined his head respectfully. "As the gentleman, it was my responsibility to ensure I planned for every eventuality. The mistakes I made were foolish when I think back now. Marcus would chastise me for my naivety. But I was just a boy, desperately trying to be a man."

"We were young and in love, of course we were naive and foolish." She took a sip of her sherry. "Do you ever wonder what our lives would have been like had your father not discovered us at the coaching inn?"

Wonder?

He had spent many hours awake at night dreaming of just that.

"We would have married, lived in a remote village far away from society's prying eyes. I would have been disowned for bringing shame on my family, forced to work to support you." It was a rather grim view, but they were the thoughts of a broken man. "Things would have been difficult, but I hope we could have been happy."

She put her hand to the base of her throat and swallowed. "I would have been happy as long as we were together."

He snorted. The contemptuous sound revealed his belief that the reality would have been so far removed from the stories told in romantic poetry. "Fate obviously had other things in store for us."

"And yet we are here together now."

He rubbed his chin as he considered her comment. A few months ago, he would have cursed and protested with uncontrollable vehemence at the mere suggestion of spending the night at her house. "Then we must be grateful for something."

A faint blush touched her cheeks. "So we have spent the last two days in each other's company, both feeling abandoned and betrayed, yet neither of us said anything."

"Pride can be both a blessing and a curse."

They fell silent. A minute passed. Isabella stared at the swirling pattern on the Persian rug, her eyes wide, glassy.

"I married Lord Fernall out of spite," she eventually said, her tone somewhat detached. "I wanted to show you that I could be a lady, someone worthy of respect. I wanted to hurt you but, in the end, I only hurt myself."

She had hurt him. The news had cut him to the bone. "But why did you leave that night? Why not wait?"

Isabella shrugged. "Lord Fernall had made your father an offer for me weeks before. Your father had not mentioned it to me as he felt I was not ready for marriage. You see, he had promised my mother he would care for me like a daughter—"

Tristan shot to his feet. Their father had insisted they treat her as kin. "Good Lord, do you think we—" He could not speak the words.

"I am not your father's daughter, Tristan." Her confident

chuckle settled his racing heart. "We were living in Italy when I was conceived."

He dropped into the chair, unable to suppress his sigh of relief. "Forgive my interruption. You were saying that my father did not think you ready for marriage."

"When he entered my chamber with your letter in his hand, he looked so lost, so forlorn. He apologised, repeatedly, cursed under his breath for having failed my mother. My heart went out to him." She put her hand to her chest. "Marrying a gentleman with a title and money seemed like the only way to appease him. Your father was a kind, quiet man, and as such did not know he was selling me to a gentleman with questionable morals."

"But you left Kempston that night."

"Lord Morford thought time away would help me to think more clearly. He wanted me to meet Lord Fernall before I made my final decision. And he knew my heart was broken, thought he was acting in the way any caring gentleman would."

Tristan raked his hand through his hair. "If only he would have come to me and questioned my motives." At the very least he had expected his father to berate him for his foolishness.

"If only I would have stayed at Kempston for one more night. If only Andrew had kept our secret." She gave a sad sigh. "Your father wanted to speak to you. But he was angry. I begged him to wait."

It was evident from Isabella's recount that his father had acted genuinely, believing his son had indeed written the letter. A wave of sadness washed over him. By the time his father returned to Kempston, Tristan was sailing to France. They had not spoken again. No doubt his father assumed his lust for adventure was the reason behind him abandoning Isabella.

"Do you believe my father was guilty of any duplicity?" From the way she had spoken, he knew the answer, but he would hear her opinion.

"No. He acted with compassion. I'm confident he had my

best interests at heart. Like me, he was perhaps blinded by Samuel's kind countenance, by his reassurances that he would be a dutiful husband."

Tristan cursed inwardly. There was only one person capable of manipulation and deception. There was only one person devious and shrewd enough to carry out such a dastardly plan—his mother.

"I know I said we should not rush back to London, but under the circumstances, I feel I must leave Highley Grange today."

Isabella caught her breath on a gasp. "Today!" A look of disappointment flashed in her brown eyes. "Can it not wait?"

Tristan shook his head. He had waited five years to discover the reason for his love's betrayal. He would not rest until the person responsible had confessed. "I must speak to my mother. I must know the part she played in all of this."

Isabella sighed, her solemn countenance tugged at his heart. "I understand."

"Come back to London with me." Logic played no part in his suggestion. But the more he thought of it, the more it made perfect sense. "Once I have spoken to my mother, we will continue our investigation into Lord Fernall's death. There is no more to be done here," he said, waving his arm about the room. "We will begin with Henry Fernall. Learn more about these sordid parties."

A smile touched the corners of her lips. "I would reside in Brook Street, of course."

His heart swelled at the prospect of them working together. Once he had made his position clear to Miss Smythe, he would be free to pay court to Isabella. "If someone did murder Lord Fernall, then we must lure them out of the shadows. Perhaps Andrew stumbled upon a piece of information, and the culprit was forced to silence him. Either way, being seen out together will soon confirm or quash the theory."

She shuffled to the edge of the chair, her excitement evident in the way she clasped her hands to her chest. "We could go to balls, the theatre, stroll through Hyde Park at the fashionable hour."

He smiled. The wild glint in her eye caused desire to flare. He had seen the same expression on the day they had eloped. A sudden and strange uneasiness settled over him. Their happiness had ended in catastrophe.

"There is every possibility the perpetrator will assume Andrew spoke to you of his suspicions," he said, his cautious tone revealing a hint of anxiety. "Should people see us together, should it become known we are asking questions, we will be leaving ourselves open to attack."

She stared at him, bit down on her bottom lip, her motionless eyes conveying she was deep in thought. "Until a few moments ago, I thought I had lost everything dear to me." She shook her head. "I cannot let you risk your life."

He sat back, rubbed his chin as he contemplated the situation. He thrived on solving puzzles. His escapades in France had served to make him stronger, given him a burning desire to see justice done.

"Let me speak to Henry Fernall, gauge his reaction." He did not want to alarm her, but a man who would stoop so low as to terrify a lady living alone was capable of far more heinous crimes. "If the staged haunting proves to be an isolated incident, then you may decide how we proceed."

It would take an immense amount of control not to grab Fernall by the throat and wring his damn neck.

"Very well." She nodded. "I must admit, even though I know Mrs. Birch is the woman in white I do not want to stay here on my own."

If he had his way, she would never be alone again. But so much had happened. There were too many lies, too many people who had conspired to keep them apart. He feared that the love they once shared—a pure, honest and genuine emotion—would now be tainted by the pain of the past.

But as a man known for his optimism all he could do was hope that, somewhere beneath the mess and the chaos, their love was not lost but lay dormant like a bud waiting for the first glimpse of spring.

# CHAPTER 12

"You're home!" The grin on his mother's face stretched from ear to ear. "How wonderful." His mother turned to the petite Miss Smythe, who was in the process of sipping her tea. "Is it not a stroke of luck, my dear?"

Tristan bowed. "Good afternoon, Miss Smythe. How fortunate that you should be here." Indeed, it saved him the trouble of calling on her. He turned his attention to her companion. "Good afternoon, Miss Hamilton."

He resisted the urge to pat the beads of sweat from his brow. Yesterday, the thirty-mile journey had taken a little over three hours in the rain. Today, with the sun shining and the road not nearly as treacherous, he had managed to reduce his time by forty minutes. Of course, anger fuelled his desire to reach his destination promptly.

Both ladies offered the perfunctory greeting.

Miss Smythe smiled sweetly. He could almost hear the birds chirping their pretty song in response. "What a pleasant surprise it is, my lord."

"Isn't it just." His mother placed her china cup on the saucer and clapped her hands. "Mr. Henderson does fret so. I often wonder as to the man's capabilities. But then Lord Morford takes his responsibilities extremely seriously. No doubt his man simply needed a little expert guidance."

Tristan groaned inwardly. He was surprised his mother had not presented his first lock of hair so they might marvel over its hue and softness as an example of utter perfection.

"I shall explain the nature of the problem once I have spoken to Miss Smythe." Tristan inclined his head. "That is if the lady is willing to accompany me on a stroll around the garden." He turned his attention to the lady in question. "Miss Hamilton may join us."

He would insist his mother remained inside. He would not give her an opportunity to snoop.

"A stroll outdoors sounds like a marvellous idea," his mother said, offering a beaming smile. "I would join you, but I cannot afford to exert myself."

"Thank you, my lord." Miss Smythe's lower lip quivered. Was the lady so timid she feared he might press his advances despite being in the company of Miss Hamilton? "A stroll would be lovely."

Aware of his mother's nose pressed against the glass of the terrace room window, Tristan escorted Miss Smythe away from the house. Miss Hamilton walked on a few feet ahead, under the guise of admiring the flowers in the lower borders.

"I love nothing more than to stand idly and smell the roses." Miss Smythe bent her head, cupped a flower between two hands and inhaled deeply. "When it comes to painting, roses are my flower of choice."

"I did not realise you enjoyed painting."

"Oh, yes. I enjoy many things. I find one's hobbies help to keep one's mind alert."

"Indeed." She really was very sweet and would be the perfect wife for the right gentleman. "While a walk is good for the constitution, my motive stems from a need to speak to you privately."

Her golden locks shimmered when caught by the sun's rays; her pleasant smile made her appear pure, angelic. "I have been waiting for an opportunity to speak to you, too, hence the reason for Miss Hamilton's eagerness to hurry on ahead."

Tristan swallowed. He hoped his intuition proved correct, and that the lady had no desire to hear a declaration of love fall from his lips. As a gentleman, he would allow the lady to address him first.

"You have my full attention," he said, aware that he should be courteous enough to intimate as to the nature of his thoughts. Should his observations prove wrong, it would save the lady any undue embarrassment. "But first, let me apologise for my mother's interference. She is often determined to get her way despite the odds."

Miss Smythe smiled. "Well, I am sure there is no harm done. Since making your acquaintance, I have found you to be rather astute. As such, I do not think it will surprise you to learn that I believe we are far too similar to make a good match."

Relief shot through him like a lightning bolt and he suppressed a satisfied grin.

"Too similar?" he asked purely as a means of clarification. To his mind, they did not share any commonalities.

"We are both far too amiable," she said. "You are kind and considerate, and I fear we would soon tire of one another."

He had struggled to be himself in her company. His impeccable manners made him nauseous. Perhaps she had no desire to discuss sewing and instead wanted a gentleman who did not nod and agree with everything she said.

How ironic.

"I know my aunt and uncle will be terribly disappointed," she continued, "but I must follow my heart."

"I fear you are right," he said in the same affable way. It

would not do to let her know he was far removed from the man she believed him to be. "My mother will be disappointed, too, of course. But we shall remain friends. Know that should you ever need assistance my door will always be open."

He had no idea why the words left his lips. He could only surmise that it had something to do with Isabella. Had there been someone else to offer her support she might never have married Lord Fernall.

"That is generous of you, my lord. One never knows what fate has in store for us. And while I doubt such a need should arise, I shall take comfort in the knowledge that I may approach you for advice."

Tristan considered mentioning Mr. Fellows, but he did not want to pry. Besides, Mr. Fellows was the epitome of amiable, and now he doubted they would suit at all. "Well, I suppose I should go and break the news to my mother."

"Then I shall bid you a good day, my lord, and quickly take my leave." Miss Smythe inclined her head. "I find your mother does not take disappointment well. Indeed, she can be rather persuasive in her methods when she is of a mind to get her way."

Tristan smiled. Miss Smythe was far more perceptive than he had given her credit.

Tristan waited for Miss Smythe to depart before returning to the terrace room. Miss Smythe's placid temperament had served to mellow his mood, albeit somewhat temporarily. One wrong word from his mother and he would struggle to keep his anger at bay.

"Well?" His mother sat forward, gripping the padded arms of her favourite chair. "Did you find her agreeable?"

Tristan sat down in the chair opposite. He wanted to rant and rage, but experience had taught him that the element of surprise, coupled with a calm reserve, worked to unnerve one's quarry.

"She is a delight," he said honestly.

"I knew if you would only give her a little time you would soon see the merits of her character."

"Indeed. I am confident Miss Smythe has the necessary attributes any gentleman would admire."

His mother gave a contented sigh. "I am truly thrilled, and what a marvellous stroke of luck you were able to return home so promptly. I hope Mr. Henderson showed some remorse for wasting your time."

He straightened, stared at the woman he knew was responsible for five years of pain and misery. "Albeit short, my trip was not a complete waste." His time at Highley Grange had proved enlightening. "But urgent business brought me back to town."

"Oh, Tristan," she said, chuckling weakly. "You may be honest with me. You came back to see Miss Smythe. I often find tiresome journeys give one the opportunity to think without distraction. I have made many wise decisions whilst rattling about the countryside in a carriage."

Wise decisions? Was that the term she used for ruining lives? "Have you ever made a decision you have later come to regret?"

She seemed a little surprised by the question. Her head wobbled as she nodded and shook it at the same time. "One must have the courage to stand by one's principles. Regret is for the weak, for those who like to wallow in sentiment."

"I suppose you're right." He gave a mocking snort. "My time in France taught me to fight for justice, to fight for those downtrodden and mistreated. A mind plagued by excessive bouts of sentimentality is of no use in the field."

She flapped her hand in the air and squeezed her eyes shut. "Let us not talk of your terrible time abroad. I cannot bear to think of you running about with those heathens."

"The point I am making is that I do not regret my time there. And you know why I left, why I had no choice but to leave Kempston, to leave England."

"Let us talk of something else." In a fluster, she patted her hair, the base of her throat, her fingers refusing to remain still. "Have you arranged to meet Miss Smythe this evening?"

"I'm to dine with an old friend this evening. Miss Smythe intends to stay at home." He felt no guilt for the small lie; it was nothing compared to the depth of his mother's deceit.

"Well, perhaps it will give Miss Smythe an opportunity to pine for you. As a wise poet once said, *always toward absent lovers love's tide stronger flows.*"

Tristan considered the quote. During his time in France, there was not a day that passed when he did not think of Isabella. Even in a state of despair, he still longed to be near her. Knowing he would see her in a few hours made his heart race.

He forced a smile. "My friend is staying at a house on Brook Street. I doubt I shall be too late home." Although if Isabella asked him to stay the night he would not refuse.

"I hope he is not staying too close to Mivart's Hotel. I've heard it can be quite noisy at night."

"You mistake me. I am not meeting a gentleman. I am dining with Lady Fernall."

The colour drained from his mother's face leaving her skin ashen, chalk-white. "Lady Fernall?"

"Indeed, I thought you might be surprised. I would have invited Isabella to dine here, but she informed me, only this morning, that you wrote to her to say she would not be welcome."

His mother opened her mouth and snapped it shut. It took but a moment for her lower lip to cease trembling and for her to call on her steely reserve for support. "I have not been well enough to receive visitors."

"Yet you received Miss Smythe and Miss Hamilton. You granted Mr. Fellows admission despite him calling at an ungodly hour. Isabella is a dear family friend."

Her nostrils flared. "So dear a friend that her meddling resulted in your brother's death."

That was not the crux of her problem with Isabella. "Andrew fell off his horse. You can hardly blame Isabella for that."

"Do you know how much time he spent there, pandering to her silly little whims?" Her white face turned a dark shade of red. "Your brother was besotted with her. Look where it got him."

Jealousy dug its long sharp claws into his heart. He sucked in a breath, determined not to let his mother's bitterness infect him too. "Andrew was so besotted he told Isabella everything that happened on the night Father forced us from the coaching inn."

His mother's resolve faltered. She gulped numerous times as though she no longer knew how to breathe air, opened her mouth to speak but the fragments of words were incoherent. "Isabella will say anything to win your affections," she finally countered.

"I know it was Andrew who wrote the letter to Isabella." It was a wild guess. There had been nothing feminine about the strong, abrupt pen strokes. It was possible Andrew could have deceived their mother. But instinct told him she was just as guilty. "He confessed to his part in the deception, and now it is time to confess to yours."

"What deception? You make it sound so distasteful. You were simply not suited. Someone had to intervene. You were young and hopelessly naive." She raised her chin and stared down her nose in a look of disgust. "Andrew did what he thought was best."

"Andrew was a jealous, spiteful prig who would sell his soul if it served his own end."

His mother sucked in a ragged breath. "How dare you speak ill of the dead."

A fiery rage coursed through him. "Then let us speak about the living. Let us discuss the part you played in it all," he said in a tone just as hostile.

"That's enough." His mother stood and banged her hand on the table. "I'll hear no more of it. I insist you leave this house at once."

Tristan smirked. "I'm afraid this is my house. If anyone is to leave here, it will be you."

He felt a faint flicker of remorse. This was not the relationship he wanted to have with his mother. His thoughts turned to Isabella, a woman with no one to care for her, a woman whose life had been ruined out of jealousy and spite.

"Leave? And where do you expect me to go?"

"Perhaps a visit to Ripon will help with your recovery. Catherine would relish the company." Indeed, his sister and her husband could share the burden.

"Ripon? Ripon!" She glared at him with burning, reproachful eyes. "That woman has poisoned your mind. Just as she did all those years ago. Just as her mother did before her."

So incensed was she that she spoke in riddles.

Tristan jumped to his feet. "Before I call for Ebsworth and instruct him to have Anna pack your trunk, tell me what you hoped to gain by your interference."

There was a brief moment of silence. The air about them swirled with an uncomfortable tension. "I would have permitted you to marry anyone of acceptable standing, anyone but her."

"But why, when she made me happy?"

"Because she is rotten to her core." His mother waved her hand in the air. "I suppose the girl cannot help her lineage."

Part of him wished he had not been desperate for an answer. The vitriolic comments falling from his mother's mouth only served to make him despise her all the more. "If you felt that way, why take her into your home?"

"I was not given the choice. Your father made a promise which he refused to renege. The man was loyal until his last breath."

"Andrew said that our father acted in good faith, that he

believed he was serving Isabella's best interests when he took her away." The lies were falling easily now. For his own sanity, he needed to believe in the goodness of one of his parents.

His mother sat down in the chair. "I'm sure it will please you to know that your father cared for Isabella and would have done anything to see her happy. Hence the reason for the letter. Hence the reason I arranged for Lord Fernall to approach him."

"But you could not have arranged anything with Lord Fernall. You knew nothing of our elopement until the day we left Kempston. There would not have been time."

She sneered. "I was not blind, Tristan. I could see what she meant to you. I spoke to Lord Fernall months before as I knew it was only a matter of time before you did something foolish. Of course, I did not expect you to behave so recklessly. I thank the Lord your brother came to me after dinner that night else God only knows where you would be now."

He would be happy, in love with his wife, a doting father to his children.

"The depth of your betrayal is sickening."

"My betrayal?" she scoffed. "I am the victim of the worst kind of deceit."

"What could possibly be worse than a mother betraying her son?"

"A husband betraying his wife," she said bluntly.

Tristan jerked his head back. "You expect me to believe my father was capable of such treachery? Are there no depths to your cruel comments and vile accusations?"

"Why do you think your father agreed to take Isabella as his ward? He would have done anything for Vivien. I have lived in that woman's shadow most of my life. Her death should have brought me some peace, but instead, it brought nothing but pain. I lost my husband. I refused to lose my son."

Time stopped for a moment.

The trauma and heartache amounted to nothing more than a woman's bitter jealousy?

Tristan dropped into the chair. "But by the very nature of your actions you have lost me, anyway," he whispered solemnly as he stared at a nondescript point beyond her shoulder. Could such a deep-rooted resentment cloud a person's judgement to the point they felt justified in all wrongdoing? "So, what are you saying? Was Isabella's mother my father's mistress?"

"Of course not," she blurted with a look of utter astonishment. "Your father was a gentleman, an upstanding member of society. He would never have degraded me in such a manner."

Tristan shook his head which only served to aggravate the pounding in his temple. "Then I do not understand your issue."

"Love, Tristan. Love. I had your father's kindness and respect, but I did not have his love. Do you know what it feels like to love someone so deeply yet know that you will never experience the same level of devotion?"

"It is devastating," he said, remembering all the lonely nights when he questioned Isabella's reasons for leaving him. "I think you forget that I have spent five years grieving for a love I thought lost to me. Your actions denied me all that you longed to have for yourself."

Anger still simmered inside. All the pain and heartache had been for naught.

"What are five years compared to a lifetime?" she replied in a tone brimming with self-pity.

There was little point trying to rationalise with a woman whose crippled heart brimmed with nothing but resentment.

"I am going out." He jumped to his feet. "You will write to Catherine and ask if you can come to Ripon. Leave the open letter on my desk as I cannot trust a word that falls from your mouth. Some time away may bring some clarity to your thoughts. The tedious carriage ride will give you time alone to consider if my father would have been so respectful to you had he been aware of your devious plot. Would any husband love a wife capable of such callous disregard for others?"

He stormed out of the room, resisted the urge to go back and demand an apology. The woman was so absorbed with herself she was oblivious to her own misdeed.

He was halfway along the hall before he heard her tottering behind him.

"Tristan! Tristan. Are you going to Brook Street? Does this mean you do not intend to offer for Miss Smythe?"

## CHAPTER 13

"I know I told you that I like to keep to country hours when I dine," Isabella said greeting Tristan in the drawing room of the house in Brook Street, "but I did not expect to see you so soon. It is only five o'clock."

"Forgive me." Tristan raked his hand through his hair and brushed the dust from the shoulders of his midnight-blue coat. "In my haste to leave the house, I have not had a chance to wash or change my clothes."

It had been a matter of hours since they had parted at Highley Grange, yet her pulse raced upon seeing him again.

"Then I shall have to see what I have done with my spare pair of breeches." Her comment was an attempt to lighten the mood. From his rigid demeanour, she could see the tension in his shoulders, knew he was trying so desperately to suppress his anger. "Mrs. Taylor has gone to fetch the tea tray, but you look as though you might be in need of something stronger." She waved to the settee. "Come. Sit down and tell me how you fared with your mother."

From the depth of his frown, she suspected the worst.

"Before I do sit, I think I will accept your offer of something more potent than tea." He scanned the drawing room, his gaze falling to the well-worn rug, to the pale yellow material covering the chair.

"I imagine it was once a rich shade of gold before someone decided to position it near the window," she said, feeling no embarrassment. "The rent reflects the rather excessive wear to the furnishings."

"At the monastery we sat on wooden benches, dined at a battered oak table, slept in a room with nothing more than a rickety metal bed. It was one of the happiest times of my life. It taught me that relationships with people are more important than relationships with objects."

She could not help but look at him with admiration. "You were never one for frivolities. It was one of the things I loved about you."

"Loved?" A smile touched the corners of his mouth. "You do not appreciate that quality now?"

"You know I do."

She did not know why she had used the past tense. Perhaps it stemmed from a need for self-preservation. He had not abandoned her. There had not been anyone else. But yet too much had happened for them to continue as they were before. They were different people now, forever changed by circumstance.

"I cannot wait to discover what other qualities of mine you admire," he said in a rich drawl.

"Oh, there are one or two," she replied coyly. "More importantly, how fussy are you when it comes to spirits?"

He raised a brow. "Please tell me you are not still talking about the ghost."

She laughed. "I am speaking about the brandy. I have no idea how long it has been sitting in the decanter."

He walked over to the drinks tray, removed the stopper from the crystal vessel and sniffed the amber liquid. "It smells like brandy." He poured a glass and took a sip, swirled it about in his mouth. "The good news is it tastes like brandy."

"Well, that is a relief," she said, pleased that his mood had mellowed slightly.

He waited for her to sit on the settee before dropping down next to her. It took an immense amount of control not to bombard him with questions. Holding her hands in her lap was the only way to prevent her restless fingers from revealing her impatience for information. One of them needed to remain calm and composed. Judging by his thin mouth and the deep furrow that had marred his brow when he'd first arrived, his mother was the one who had deceived them.

Swallowing a mouthful of liquor, he shook visibly. "There is no pleasant way of saying this, and so I shall come straight to the point." He sucked in a breath. "Andrew wrote the letter purporting to be from me and together with my mother conspired to deceive both you and my father." The words were said too quickly as though to hold on to them would only serve to cause him more pain.

There was a brief moment of silence.

"It is as we suspected then." The ache in her chest could be attributed to sadness as opposed to anger. She had come to forgive Andrew, value his friendship, yet his part in the charade tainted everything. "Did your mother say why they chose to ruin our lives?"

"I can only assume Andrew's involvement stemmed from jealousy. Perhaps he imagined himself in love with you and so sought a means to force us apart."

Andrew had always been very attentive to her, cared for her in a way an older brother might. "I know your mother wanted him to marry. He once told me she would never approve of the woman he had chosen. But he never gave me any indication he favoured me."

Tristan gave a contemptuous snort. "Andrew preferred to use

covert methods. He would have won your love as a friend first, lured you into a situation where you would have struggled to refuse him." He paused, opened his mouth to speak but then shook his head.

"We have lived with other people's lies and deceit," she said in response to his hesitance. "Trust me enough to know that we may always speak freely to one another without fear of censure or reprisal. Honesty is the only way forward."

He acknowledged her comment with a curt nod. "I fear, had Andrew discovered any information proving that your ... that Lord Fernall was murdered, you would have been forever in his debt. A man capable of betraying his kin so easily is equally capable of blackmail."

Isabella sighed.

She didn't want to believe it of Andrew but in her heart knew Tristan spoke the truth. "You have given a possible motive for Andrew's treachery, but what is your mother's excuse for such diabolical behaviour?"

He drained his glass, placed it on the octagonal mahogany table next to him before taking her hand in his. "She thought that my father was in love with your mother. She knew it was a purely platonic relationship, but bitterness taints my mother's thoughts and feelings. Even now, she feels justified in her methods to keep us apart."

The truth was like a knife to her heart.

Surely it amounted to more than an act of jealousy.

"Your father visited both my parents many times over the years," she said in an attempt to make sense of it all. "He gave my mother support when my father died, promised to care for me if ever I was left alone. Never once did I think there was anything more to their relationship."

Tristan patted her hand gently. "My father was a loyal husband by all accounts. I think that is what hurts my mother the most. True love is rare, precious. She craved it, avoided anything that reminded her of her failings."

"Please tell me you do not pity her." The sudden surge of anger caught her by surprise. "There is no justification for what she did to us."

He gripped her hand tightly. "You mistake me. I am merely trying to establish her thought process. I will never forgive her for her meddling."

A light tap on the door announced Mrs. Taylor's arrival with the tea tray. The housekeeper placed it carefully on the side table.

"Thank you, Mrs. Taylor," Isabella said. "You may leave us. I shall pour."

"My mother's actions did not bring her the peace she so desperately sought," Tristan said as Mrs. Taylor closed the door behind her. "Indeed, it pains her to think of what I did whilst in France."

"She drove you away. What did she expect you to do?"

Tristan shrugged. "No doubt she assumed I would find someone else to marry."

Isabella's heart lurched at the thought. "Then I am grateful you decided to work for a living instead."

"You know, with my penchant for work, perhaps we should go into business together."

"A viscount in business?" She chuckled, relieved to have moved on to another subject. All talk of ghosts, murder and deception made her heart feel heavy. "What sort of business?"

His wicked grin caused her stomach to flip. "Wouldn't you like to spend your days working with me? We could open an agency that deals in the solving of mysteries. Of course, the working hours would be long."

"Don't tell me, we would be required to spend our nights together, too," she said, eager to respond to his playful tone.

He moistened his lips. "Ghosts rarely appear during the daylight hours. I thought you would know that."

As ridiculous as the idea sounded, she welcomed any opportunity to spend more time with him. "I suppose we would have premises where we would greet prospective clients, rooms above to rest when we cannot keep our eyes open after a hectic night."

"A hectic night," he repeated, his voice silky smooth. "You make work sound so appealing."

It did sound wonderful and exciting. "Well, we have one more mystery of our own to solve before we can even begin to think of doing so in a professional capacity," she said to quash all unrealistic thoughts. Daydreams, whilst entertaining, only served to bring disappointment. "But I have been thinking. Now we know the haunting has nothing to do with Samuel's death, and that I was never in any real danger, there is a part of me that wonders if his falling down the stairs was an accident after all."

"On the surface, that is what it would seem." He nodded when she gestured to the tea tray. "I am inclined to think the same about Andrew's accident, too. However, we have nothing to lose by asking a few questions, or by prying a little into Lord Fernall's affairs."

With a firm grip on the china saucer, she handed him his tea. "So you still agree we should be seen out together?" There was a nervous hitch in her voice that she could not suppress. "You do not care what people think?"

"There is no need to sound so terrified at the prospect. You're a widow. I am not beholden to anyone. We may do as we please. By God, we have waited long enough to spend time in each other's company."

"Whilst no one knows of our attempted elopement, there will be gossip. People will assume I am your mistress." The thought caused a sensual beat between her thighs. It had been so long since she had felt the intoxicating thrum of desire. The last time was in her youth. In her innocence, the feeling had not burned with the same intensity.

"Does the thought offend you?" His heated gaze drifted slowly over her face, scanned her grey dress as though it was made from the finest gossamer and proved utterly scandalous.

"I am used to sly whispers as I walk by, used to turned-up noses and direct cuts. To be thought your mistress carries more prestige than to be known as the wife who tolerated her husband's obscene parties, or a wife capable of murder."

"Whilst I recognise the compliment infused within your words, know that I could never demean you in such a way."

What was he saying? Did he not want her? Did he not feel the same urgent need clawing in his belly? Would he ever learn to love her again, love her enough to make her his wife?

An awkward silence ensued.

The nature of their relationship was complex. Once, they had loved each other deeply. It had been a pure love. Sweet. Hardly innocent. She had given herself to him on the night before they had eloped. The moment of their joining had roused feelings of utter bliss. Now, despite believing her heart was but a pit of cold, charred embers, the fiery flickers of desire sparked and burned anew.

Perhaps they could fall in love again. All she could do was hope.

"Well, we will ignore the gossips," she said, feeling a renewed sense of determination to win his heart. "After a wretched few months, we deserve some enjoyment."

A smile touched the corners of his mouth, and his brilliant blue eyes glistened. "The Holbrooks are hosting a ball tomorrow evening. It is said to be an event to surpass all others. I'm told everyone will be there. It will be the perfect opportunity for me to speak to Henry Fernall."

If it was to be such an elaborate soiree why had she not heard of it? "What deems it to be so special? Will there be acrobats and jugglers?"

He shook his head. "There is to be a card game. The stakes will be high. The night will end in rejoicing for some, disaster for others. Whilst the matrons would ordinarily disapprove, people will speak of the winners and losers for years to come."

"And no one would want to admit they were not there to witness such a momentous event."

"Precisely. In light of what tragedies will come to pass, I doubt many will take notice of us dancing together."

Her heart fluttered up to her throat. He intended to take her in his arms then. "I cannot recall the last time I took to the floor. There is every chance I will step on your toes."

"Then I shall just have to hold you a little tighter than would be appropriate."

"And how tight would that be?" Carried along on a buoyant wave of euphoria, she found it impossible not to continue their amorous banter.

He leant forward and placed his cup on the tray. "Perhaps I should show you. It would not do for you to gasp in shock when we are trying to remain inconspicuous." He stood and held out his hand.

She glanced at it for a moment, noted that the skin was not as soft and smooth as she remembered. His work in France must have required an element of physical strength. An image of his muscular torso flashed into her mind. She did not need to glance in the mirror to know a blush touched her cheeks.

"I presume you mean to lead me in a waltz," she said as she slid her hand slowly into his. A soft gasp breezed from her lips. The sudden tingling in her palm and the rush of hot blood racing up her arm caught her off guard.

"You see," he said with a satisfied smile as he led her to a spot where there was more space. "Such a pleasurable sound is sure to make people stare." He wrapped his arm around her waist, made no attempt to hold a perfect line as he pulled her close.

"I think people would gape if we stood this close." His coat skimmed her dress. The taut muscles in his legs brushed against her thighs. As he hummed a triple-beat rhythm, they swayed back and forth, round and round. "It feels positively indecent." The sudden rush of excitement made her giddy.

"Am I to assume from your playful tone that you approve of my attempt at indecency?" The undeniable sensuality in his words held her captive.

"Can you not hear my approval when I catch my breath?" She could feel all control slipping. She relished being so intimate with him. "Can you not see it reflected in my eyes?"

He stared into her eyes as they moved together. In his, she saw a look of longing, a smouldering passion that roused an ache deep in her core.

"Do you want me to tell you what I see in your eyes?" he said in a husky tone.

Her broad smile conveyed the happiness she felt inside. "Please do."

"I see the young woman I once knew. I see the same vibrant vivacity that always held me spellbound. I see the woman I am yearning to know again, a woman whose potent allure draws me, a woman I cannot live without."

Isabella choked back a sob. She never thought to hear such beautiful words from him again. She never thought she would ever feel so adored. "Make me yours, Tristan." The words tumbled from her mouth without thought or censure.

*Make me feel clean; make me feel whole.*

But she did not give him a chance to respond. Giving in to the craving that clawed away inside, she pressed her lips to his as though she would die without his touch.

# CHAPTER 14

*T*he kiss felt different from the one they had shared at Highley Grange. There was something raw, something possessive about the way she claimed his mouth.

By God, he was not complaining.

Her lips were so hot, soft as silk as they moved sensually over his. He drew her close. The desperate need burning within threatened to consume him. Blood rushed to his cock, fast, furious, the throbbing ache growing in intensity until the desire to bury himself deep inside her became unbearable.

He had never needed her like he did at that moment.

The thought forced a groan from the depths of his throat, and he coaxed her plump flesh apart with his tongue to penetrate her mouth. Pure carnal lust ripped through him. His heart swelled until he feared it might burst from his chest.

"God, I have waited so long to taste you," he panted as they broke to catch their breath. "I will die if I don't have you."

She stepped back out of his grasp. The loss of her warm body made him want to cry out in despair, the pain growing unbearable when she walked over to the door.

"I have waited a lifetime to feel your touch, too." She turned the key in the lock. "And I can wait no longer."

As she swung back around to face him, she wore her desire like her masquerade mask: with confidence, with pride. Her eyes sparkled like the dark jewels beneath the candlelight. Her aura held the same magnetic quality as it had done that night. Yet there was one intrinsic difference. As she came to stand before him, her lips were curved up into a bright smile.

Bloody hell.

He wanted to spend his whole life making her happy.

When he held out his hands, she hurried into his arms. They embraced for a few seconds, clung on to each other, their breathless pants evidence of what this moment meant to both of them.

"Know I will never desert you," he whispered as he rained kisses along the elegant line of her jaw. "You will never be alone again."

She closed her eyes, tilted her neck to one side to allow him easier access. "Tell me I am not dreaming. Tell me you're really here, that I will not wake to find the last few days never existed."

With trembling hands he cupped her face, revelled in the smoothness of her skin. "Trust me. It is a dream. One I have spent many restless nights imagining. But dreams do come true, Isabella." He bent his head and traced the line of her lips with his tongue. "Does that not feel real?"

"Yes." The word was but a whispered sigh.

He kissed her deeply, their tongues dancing slowly and elegantly at first, building in intensity until reaching a crescendo of wild thrusts, whimpers and groans. Rampant hands grappled for some way to ease the flames roaring within.

"I have never stopped wanting you," she said, pushing his coat from his shoulders until it fell to the floor. "I never expected to know your body again."

He fiddled with his cravat, angled his head so he still had access to her mouth. His waistcoat joined the pile on the thread-

136

bare rug. But before he could drag his shirt off his back, delicate hands found their way beneath the fine lawn to caress the hard planes.

"Isabella." Her name left his lips as he closed his eyes and let his head fall back. Every part of him responded to the touch of her hot hands. He gulped as they drifted down to the fall of his breeches.

"Tell me the truth," she whispered, her voice rich, luxurious as she stroked the evidence of his arousal through the material. "Have you truly saved yourself all these years?"

*Saved* was not the word he would use. He had starved himself, and she was the only woman capable of satisfying his hunger. Indeed, he felt no shame for his lack of experience.

"It was always you." His desire spiralled. "It was only ever you."

She reacted instantly to his words, claiming his mouth as though she, too, was famished beyond measure.

"I am empty inside without you." She broke contact to fiddle with the buttons on her dress, gestured for him to offer his assistance.

With his mind lost in a blissful blur he undressed her, stripped her bare and almost expired from her blinding beauty. Every luscious curve was as he remembered.

He dragged his shirt over his head with such vigour he feared he might tear the fine lawn. "I have a feeling this will be … will be a cumbersome affair." He struggled to form coherent words. "God, I cannot wait a moment longer."

He pulled her into his arms, captured her mouth, his tongue delving deep inside where it was warm and wet. The feel of her soft skin against his chest heightened his arousal. Her fingers found their way into the hair above his nape; the gentle tug made him swell and pulse with need.

"I need you now," he muttered against her deliciously divine lips.

Her fingers travelled slowly down the front of his chest until she reached the band of his breeches. "Then we must do something about these," she said with a smirk. "And do you intend to wear your boots? Will it not be a little uncomfortable?"

Damn it all. He felt like a boy fresh from the schoolroom. "I want you so badly I have lost all use of my faculties."

Her sweet giggle made his cock twitch. "Sit down. Let me help you."

He dropped into the nearest chair as requested, watched with fascination as her sumptuous breasts wobbled with each tug of his boot. There was something erotic about the way she undressed him, something alluring about her lack of embarrassment. Indeed, he rather suspected she enjoyed the way he devoured her body with just his eyes.

When his cock sprang free of his breeches, she clambered up to sit astride him. "You've had a tiring day." The sweet timbre of her voice fuelled his desire. "Let me ease your tension."

He expected her to rain kisses along the line of his jaw, to stroke the muscles in his chest with slow sensual caresses. He did not expect her to wrap her dainty fingers around his throbbing cock, to guide him into position and sink slowly down until she had taken the full length of him.

"Bloody hell."

A long, pleasurable sigh left her lips. "Oh, we have waited so long for this," she whispered as she began to ride him.

He gripped the soft flesh at her hips, forced his eyes to stay open as he did not want to miss a single second.

"Do you mind that I have taken the lead?" She rolled her hips and took him deeper into her core, her full breasts coming but a few inches from his mouth.

"Hell, no. I am yours. You may do what you want with me."

A whimper left her lips when he moved his hands to caress her breasts, the pad of his thumb grazing the hard pink nipples.

He wanted to lavish the peaks with his tongue, but he would have a lifetime to explore her body.

He watched her with a feeling of wonder. Her rich brown eyes smouldered with an intensity that stole his breath. His restless hands moved over her body, stroking the sweet flesh at the apex of her thighs until her eyes glazed, until she trembled and cried out his name.

"Oh, Tristan. I … I have missed you."

Damn. The sight of her body quivering with the effects of her release was so magnificent he doubted he would last much longer. Indeed, as her tight muscles pulsed around his length, he knew he would have to move.

Rousing all the strength he could muster, he held her to his damp body, stood and then lowered her down to the floor.

The first thrust, as she wrapped her legs around his waist, caused a guttural groan to burst from his lips. He thought to take his time, to savour every moment, but the urge to pound into her, again and again, took hold.

Digging her fingernails into his buttocks, she spurred him on, drove him long and hard until beads of sweat trickled down his spine, until the moist sound of their joining was sweet music to his ears.

"Don't stop." Her breath breezed over him. "Don't ever stop loving me."

His heart swelled to gargantuan proportion, the rush of blood filling his cock until he was about ready to burst. "I … I need to withdraw," he gasped though he was reluctant to leave her warm, wet body.

"Must you?"

Good Lord. He would love nothing more than to spill his seed inside her—to claim her, to make her his, to find a way to cement their souls together for all eternity.

But he was not a selfish man.

Suppressing a groan of disappointment he took himself in

hand, though she continued to stroke and caress him until he shuddered with the power of his release.

Struggling to catch his breath, he collapsed on top of her. She wrapped her arms and legs around him and held him tight. As his mind cleared, he took a moment to say a silent prayer of thanks, an expression of gratitude for the force of fate that had worked to bring them together.

They remained in the drawing room for another hour, moved to her bedchamber once they had found the energy to climb the stairs. They ate in her chamber. He loved her into the early hours. Their joining, whilst carnal, conveyed a depth of tenderness and emotion that touched his soul.

"Happiness feels so much more profound when you have experienced sadness," she mused.

He trailed his fingers over the curve of her hip as they lay naked on the bed. "I never thought to feel this way again," he said, acknowledging the truth to her words. "It has always been you. I know I will never feel this way with another."

She smiled, caressed his cheek as she stared into his eyes. "Then we will let nothing keep us apart."

# CHAPTER 15

The line of carriages stretched all the way along the length of Wigmore Street and once around the circular gardens in the centre of Cavendish Square. A man with nothing better to do could have counted their number which was sure to reach fifty or more.

Tristan was grateful he had chosen to walk. There was little point scanning the row of conveyances looking for Isabella. A grey mist hung in the air like a grimy veil, blurring the lines, so one had to squint to see anything clearly. The drivers' cries cut through the smoky air as they attempted to ward others away from jumping the queue. Carriage doors opened and slammed shut. Hazy black shadows swarmed the pavement as gentlemen decided to abandon their vehicles and walk.

In stark contrast to the gloomy atmosphere outside, the interior of the Holbrooks' ballroom was so bright it was blinding. Mirrors stretching from floor to ceiling covered the walls between the long windows. The reflection of numerous chandeliers enhanced the brilliant ambiance. The pale blue and gilt decor gave a light, airy appearance despite there being far too many people packed into the decadent room.

Walking over to the terrace doors, as that was where he had told Isabella he would wait, Tristan was shocked to see Matthew Chandler propped up against a white marble statue of a naked Grecian goddess.

"I thought you were in Bedfordshire." Chandler straightened and gave an arrogant grin. "Did your business prove unsatisfying?"

Tristan smiled. "Not at all. I managed to achieve a great deal in the space of a relatively short period." He glanced at the double doors leading into the ballroom, anticipating Isabella's arrival. "Let us just say that my mood is much improved since I last saw you."

"Ah, I see. You are waiting for someone." Chandler missed nothing.

"Perhaps." Tristan was deliberately vague as he knew his friend thrived on intrigue. "I assume you're here for the card game."

"Why would you think that?" Chandler said with a smirk. "No. I am here to ravish a wallflower in the hope she'll marry me and fund my penchant for reckless gambling."

The gentleman had no shame. "You're here for the gambling, though I suspect that will be the extent of your activities this evening."

Chandler raised an arrogant brow. "One never knows when good fortune may strike. In an hour, I could be celebrating a great victory and then I shall have no choice but to find a pleasurable way to channel my excitement."

Tristan snorted. "Or you may drown your sorrows in a bottle of brandy whilst cradling a loaded pistol in your lap."

Chandler brushed his hand through his mop of black hair. "It would never come to that. There are plenty of ways to recoup one's losses without resorting to desperate measures." He glanced up at the statue's bare marble breasts. "It may require selling my soul to a lonely widow or two."

Tristan chuckled, amazed that the gentleman could be so calm whilst anticipating such a dire outcome. "I doubt it will be your soul that you'll be selling."

Chandler laughed, too. "As you're so jovial this evening, am I to assume you are eager to be reunited with Isabella? I cannot help but wonder what has happened in the space of three days to alter your mood."

It occurred to him that his friend could prove to be a useful ally in his investigation. Chandler knew the sordid habits of many gentlemen of the *ton*. "You are well aware I did not go to Bedfordshire."

Chandler slapped his hand to his chest in surprise but could not hide his wicked grin. "Then where the blazes have you been?"

Tristan glanced back over his shoulder. "Hoddesdon."

"Hoddesdon? You mean the village on the road to Cambridge?"

"Isabella lives at Highley Grange, but half a mile from there." Tristan hesitated. If Marcus were here, he would caution him about trusting a man he had not seen for five years. "Can I trust you, Matthew?" he asked, although he already knew the answer.

Chandler jerked his head back in surprise. "You should not have to ask the question. I am not a gentleman who needs friends or companions. I told you once that I would never forget what you did for me, and I meant it."

Tristan put his hand on Chandler's shoulder. "There is a reason Isabella sought me out. She believes someone may have murdered her husband. My brother, Andrew, was travelling from Hoddesdon when he fell from his horse and broke his neck. She thinks both incidents are connected."

Chandler rubbed his chin. "Or are both unfortunate accidents and she wanted an excuse to be alone with you?"

The mere thought of being alone with Isabella roused the memory of their passionate coupling.

"There is more to the whole situation than that," he said, scrambling around in his mind as he tried to find the best way to tell his friend that he had been chasing ghosts. "Isabella has been the victim of foul play. Whilst at Highley Grange we discovered that Henry Fernall arranged for the servants to frighten her into believing the house was haunted. Indeed, she had taken a house in Brook Street for fear of going home."

Chandler nodded slowly as he absorbed the information. "And so now you wonder as to Henry's motive. Now, you wonder if the accidents are in some way related."

"Precisely. Do not mistake me. Isabella told me about her husband's sordid parties." God, he hated referring to Lord Fernall as her husband. "I can only presume to imagine what sort of things went on there."

"You know I am always the first in line when it comes to seeking pleasure," Chandler said, his mouth curling up into a wicked grin. "But I cannot understand what is enjoyable about hiding in a secret room to watch unsuspecting couples grunt and groan."

Tristan jerked his head back, blinked rapidly as he replayed Chandler's words over again in his mind. "You mean you know about the secret room in the bedchamber?" He grasped Chandler's elbow and pulled him into the alcove for he strained to hear whilst the orchestra were playing in full flow. "Why the hell didn't you tell me?"

Chandler shrugged. "I did not think it important. It is certainly not a secret amongst the more dissipated echelons of the *ton*. It is why I was more inclined to believe he met his end at the hands of a disgruntled guest as opposed to his wife."

Tristan raked his hand through his hair in frustration. "Lord Fernall was alone with Isabella when he died. There is no way to prove someone else was involved."

"Had it not been for Henry's involvement I would have told you to forget about Lord Fernall. You've spent five years pining for a lost love. Now you have found each other again you deserve to find some happiness." Chandler sighed. "But even my inert instincts tell me something isn't quite right."

Tristan thought so, too. The niggling doubt in the back of his mind refused to be tempered. What if Andrew had discovered something sinister? What if he ignored his intuition and something untoward happened to Isabella?

"Have you heard any rumours regarding Henry Fernall?" Tristan had never been one to pay much attention to gossip.

"He doesn't gamble. Well, we do not frequent the same establishments, and I have not heard tales of unpaid debt." Chandler pursed his lips. "Mrs. Forester is his mistress. Some say he is besotted with the woman, but I find he always has a look on his face that shows displeasure in most things."

Relief flooded Tristan's chest. He had feared Henry Fernall's intention was to make Isabella his mistress. Why else would he have wanted her to live at Grangefields? Unless he intended to use Highley Grange for another purpose.

Chandler's sharp and sudden intake of breath broke his reverie. "Well, well." Chandler's wide eyes focused on a point in the distance. "It appears you are not the only one to return from your trip thoroughly transformed."

Tristan followed Chandler's curious gaze, raising himself up on his toes as he scanned the tightly packed throng. A vibrant burst of yellow caught his attention as a few gasps of surprise drifted through the charged air.

"Most people believe yellow to be an ostentatious colour," Chandler mused in a tone reminiscent of the night they had observed Isabella at the masquerade. "Some would say it suggests the wearer is rather pretentious and self-absorbed."

The smile on Tristan's face as he watched Isabella approach masked the sudden rush of lustful desire. He had expected her to wear grey or some other equally dull colour. With her delicate curves encased in the smooth satin, she sparkled with a vivacious sensuality. The hairs at his nape sprung to attention. The tiny receptors sent tingles and shivers shooting down his spine.

"Are you not the least bit interested to hear more?" Chandler added in a bid to capture his attention.

"Come then. I know you are dying to give me your opinion."

Chandler folded his arms across his chest. "I say it creates an air of excitement. It suggests a sensual vitality that robs a man of his breath."

It certainly did that. The woman before him brought to mind images of scorching hot sunny days and lush summer meadows, yet his thoughts turned dark and downright wicked.

"She is utterly captivating," he said as his heart hammered in his chest.

"Indeed," Chandler agreed. "Does she know that you're still in love with her?"

The question forced him to turn his head. "I thought you were a gentleman who shies away from any expression of sentiment." Tristan refused to deny what he knew to be true.

Chandler shrugged. "I make the odd exception. You should know I am a man who rallies for the downtrodden. I'm a man who hopes some poor, destitute gentleman wins a fortune tonight that will irrevocably alter the course of his life. You and Isabella belong together. You always have."

"I was lucky to have you to confide in all those years ago," Tristan said. During the years spent at Harrow and Cambridge, Chandler had been his constant companion.

A gentleman in a green velvet coat approached. He gave a mumbled introduction before whispering in Matthew Chandler's ear. The man nodded several times upon hearing Chandler's reply before scurrying off into the crowd.

Tristan stepped forward as Isabella emerged to stand before him. He wanted desperately to take her hands in his and pull her close. "You look divine," he said, aware that his breath came far too quickly. "I thought we said it would be wise to remain inconspicuous. You light up the room like a brilliant beacon." He dabbed the corner of his mouth. "My excessive salivating will soon be cause for concern."

Her broad smile caused another jolt of awareness. "It seems there is no longer a reason for me to hide behind a shroud of sadness. I have not worn this gown for years," she patted the material at her stomach, "and am somewhat shocked to find I can fit into it."

Chandler cleared his throat. "Excuse me for interrupting, but I must take my leave. The game is to start shortly."

Tristan patted his friend on the arm. "Then I shall pray that the night brings good fortune."

"Lady Fernall," Chandler said, offering a graceful bow. "After the bout of miserable weather, I am pleased to see the sun is shining once again."

Isabella brushed her hand down the front of her satin gown. "It is a time to rejoice, is it not, Mr. Chandler?"

"Indeed it is."

As Chandler moved away through the crowd, Tristan touched Isabella's fingers discreetly. "I cannot begin to tell you how much I want you." His rich tone conveyed the depth of his desire.

A faint blush touched her cheeks. "I thought we were not supposed to draw any undue attention to ourselves."

He glanced at her vivid gown and smiled. He wanted nothing more than to forget about the Fernalls, his mother and everyone else who sought to keep them apart. To cover her body, to bury himself inside the only woman he had ever wanted, was the prominent thought in his mind.

"Then let us return to Brook Street, lock the door and say to hell with the world." It was wishful thinking on his part, but the sudden hitch in her breath told him it was what she wanted, too.

She smiled, raised her hand to touch his cheek but then stopped. "When we are done with this mess, when we can put it all behind us, then we will be free to begin again."

"After all that occurred between us last night, perhaps we might skip breakfast and tiffin and move straight to dessert."

Isabella batted him on the arm. "You really are so adorable when you're in a playful mood."

He feigned disappointment. "I don't want to be adorable. Dogs are adorable. I want you to crave me with a passion that makes you giddy."

She stared into his eyes; the heated look seared his soul. "If I made you party to my thoughts, we would achieve nothing this evening. But I will find a way to show my gratitude for all your help."

Her words were enough to focus his mind on the task ahead. If it took all night, he would leave with answers. Then he could dedicate his time to more pleasurable pursuits.

"Then we must devise a plan of action," he said, rousing enthusiasm.

She bit down on her bottom lip before saying, "I think I should be the one to talk to Henry. He noticed me arrive—"

"I should imagine everyone noticed you arrive. But perhaps I should speak to him. I'm impartial and so can be more objective." He knew as soon as the comment left his lips that *impartial* was the last word he would use to describe the depth of his involvement.

"I disagree." She raised her chin in protest. "One word from his arrogant mouth and I fear you will not be able to contain yourself."

Isabella was right, of course. He wanted to throttle the man for terrifying a woman half out of her wits.

"Very well." He nodded despite feeling some apprehension. "But focus on the reason he found it necessary to torment you.

Tell him all you know about the hauntings but mention nothing of his father's death."

She nodded. "What will you do?"

"I shall hide behind a planter and watch you."

"Oh, I will not be able to focus if I can feel your gaze upon me. You can trust me, Tristan. I shall not leave this room."

He trusted her; Henry Fernall was another matter.

"Then I will wander about the ballroom. I may even go and watch the card game for a while if they allow spectators." Matthew Chandler would need someone of sound mind to drag him from the table before he lost everything he owned. Besides, Chandler was a fountain of knowledge when it came to the habits of his peers. No doubt he knew some juicy *on dit* that would prove enlightening. "But before you go, you should know Henry has a mistress, a Mrs. Forester. It might be important."

"A mistress? How intriguing."

"Apparently, he is thought to be besotted with her."

"I assume she is a widow?" When he shrugged in response, she added, "Then our conversation might prove interesting."

A sudden wave of anxiety gripped him. "If we cannot find each other in the crush, we should meet on the terrace."

She placed her gloved hand on his arm. "Agreed."

The heat from her palm brought a measure of comfort. "I shall wait for you," he said as she turned to walk away.

He would wait a lifetime.

## CHAPTER 16

*I*sabella found Henry Fernall conversing with a group of gentlemen in the corridor leading out of the ballroom. He had his back to her, but she would know his sloping shoulders anywhere.

Catching the attention of a portly gentleman as she approached, he inclined his head. The action caused Henry to turn around. His mouth curved fractionally at the corners, the weak expression of pleasure lasted for all but a few seconds.

After turning back to bid the men farewell, he walked towards her. "Isabella. You should have sent word you were attending this evening. I would have escorted you." He scanned her gown with some curiosity. "I do not think I have ever seen you looking so radiant. Are you here alone?"

She chose to ignore his question. "I have just returned to town after a short spell at Highley Grange."

His face remained as expressionless as an artist's blank canvas. "I trust everything was in order. I'm afraid I have kept Mr. Blackwood busy with the renovations to the townhouse. Mrs. Birch knows to send word should any problems arise."

"It is my recent visit to Highley Grange that forced me to

150

seek you out." She was rather proud that she had managed to remain so calm and composed. "I understand that now is perhaps not the best time to discuss the strange events that occurred there. But it is a matter of some importance, and therefore cannot wait."

"Strange events? Has something untoward happened? Has one of the staff been taken ill?"

Oh, he really was exceptional when it came to deceiving others.

A commotion at the end of the long corridor captured their attention. A rather scrawny-looking gentleman ambled out of the room to their right. He grabbed the arm of the chair propped against the wall outside but it failed to stop him from falling to his knees. Trembling fingers reached out to loosen the knot in his cravat. The man's death-like pallor made her suck in a breath.

"Should someone not go over and help him?" she said in a sudden panic as people simply stared at the distressing spectacle. "It appears as though his heart has given out."

Henry gave a disdainful sneer. "It is not his heart that's weak but his morals."

Tristan had mentioned a card game. Was this gentleman a casualty of the high stakes at play?

"I am certain those people standing gaping are guilty of some immoral act," she said, for Henry was a hypocrite of monumental proportion. "Should we not show him some compassion?"

"Not at all. It serves the blighter right. No doubt he has just gambled his inheritance and lost. If he has any sense, he'll pack a trunk full of valuables and be on the first ship to Boston."

Isabella had heard many tales of ruination, but to witness it firsthand? The look of utter despair marring the fellow's face reminded her of how reckless and foolish people could be.

A footman dressed in fine livery exited the room, lifted the man to his feet and escorted him to another room further along the corridor.

"I hope the footman will stay with him until he recovers," she said, though she struggled to convey a hint of optimism.

"Judging by the look on his face, recovery is far from an option." Henry shook his head and turned to face her. "Now, before the rude interruption you were about to explain the strange occurrences at Highley Grange."

A busy thoroughfare was not the place to discuss the terrifying events he had orchestrated to frighten her. Nor would it do to be seen entering a room alone with him.

With a huff to express her frustration, she moved to the alcove opposite in the hope it would afford a little privacy. "I cannot stay at Highley Grange another night," she said as he came to stand before her.

"After all that has gone on there in the past, I do not know how you can bear to cross the threshold." Henry flicked the lock of brown hair from his brow in such a way as to convey his irritation.

"It is not the past that concerns me. I fear the place is haunted." She scrutinised his face. Still, he showed not a single sign of guilt, not a glimmer of remorse for his wicked betrayal.

"Then you must come and live at Grangefields." He made no mention of ghosts. Not even to scoff at the idea. Instead, his lips thinned in a look of reproof. "I do not know why you have not done so sooner. You would have a suite for your own personal use. You would be free to use the townhouse when I am not in residence if you would prefer it so."

She wondered if he was about to offer her a golden carriage and a team of matching pairs. Why did he want her to leave Highley Grange so desperately? Perhaps a penchant for wild parties was in the blood. Perhaps he had inherited his father's problem in the bedchamber.

But then she remembered his mistress, Mrs. Forester.

"What will I do when you marry? Surely your wife will not want a stepmother living in the house, particularly when we are the same age."

He shrugged dismissively. "But I do not intend to wed. At least, not in the foreseeable future. You would be free to live at Grangefields without fear of being disturbed."

How interesting.

She frowned. "Some people say your affection for your mistress, Mrs. Forester, is the reason you avoid the debutantes and have no desire to wed."

It was though a sudden volatile wind had swept in to swirl ominously around them. Henry's stone-cold expression sent a shiver racing through her.

"Where did you hear that?" he demanded, the tiny twitch in his cheek being the only visible evidence of anger. "Who told you such a thing?"

Isabella raised one shoulder in a casual shrug. "I heard in mentioned in the retiring room by a group of ladies at a ball a few days ago. I heard Mrs. Birch talking to Molly. Indeed, just this evening, two gentlemen were discussing your relationship with your mistress."

Henry was a private man who could not abide people prying into his affairs. The thought of being the topic of conversation amongst gossips would not sit well with him.

"Then you should know not to listen to those who have nothing better to do than prod and poke others for information." His thin mouth curled down in a look of disgust and contempt.

Excellent! Any expression of emotion conveyed a weakened stance.

"So are you saying Mrs. Forester is not your mistress?" She raised a curious brow. "Are you saying they are all mistaken?"

"I refuse to discuss my private affairs with you or with anyone."

"Well, I understand your concern when it comes to gossips.

Equally, it would not do for others to discover that ghosts wander the corridors of Highley Grange. Not when you mean to sell."

It took all the control she possessed not to snigger.

"Sell? Why on earth would you think I want to sell Highley Grange?"

"To pay off your mounting debts, of course." She cast him her sweetest smile. "If only you would have told me that is the real reason for wanting me to move to Grangefields. As your stepmother, you must know I would have supported your decision."

He detested her referring to herself as his stepmother. It suggested a level of superiority he refused to accept or acknowledge.

The faint sound of grinding teeth resonated from behind his pursed lips. He glanced back over his shoulder, looked to the left and then the right before giving her his full attention.

"I am not in debt. Do not dare think to compare me to the bunch of mindless degenerates sitting in that room." He jerked his head in the direction of the door at the end of the corridor. "Whilst my father had many faults, his ability to deal with fiscal matters was not one of them. Only a fool would fritter away his inheritance."

Isabella sighed. "Then it does not make any sense."

"What does not make sense?"

"If you do not need to sell Highley Grange, why would you arrange for the servants to hide in the secret room only to come out at night to scare me out of my wits?" Her high-pitched tone revealed a trace of anger.

"Keep your voice down," he whispered. "These hauntings have obviously played havoc with your sensibilities. Why would the servants do such a thing? The mind is a fragile thing. But you do not have to go back there. I shall send Mr. Blackwood to collect your belongings so that you may move to Grangefields. I am rarely ever there, so you do not need to worry on that score."

The gentleman's urgency to see her leave her home conveyed nothing but desperation.

"But you despise gossip." She kept her voice calm, chose not to mention that some would assume they were conducting a liaison. "What do you think people will say when they discover I have moved back to Grangefields?" Despite his pleas, she had no intention of doing so, of course. "I cannot say it is because my house is haunted. They would think me fit for Bedlam."

He waved his hand in frustration. "It is simple. You will say that you refuse to live in a house used for immoral purposes and have decided to move to Grangefields until alternative arrangements can be made. After what went on in that house, there is not a person in the land who would argue with your logic."

Henry appeared to have thought of everything. Hidden beneath his now cool façade she sensed a frisson of excitement. He was a gentleman who liked to get his way, and he obviously felt he was making progress.

"But that still does not explain why you instructed the servants to play vile tricks on me. I cannot even begin to describe some of the horrors I have witnessed."

He inhaled deeply. "As I have already said—"

"Mrs. Birch confessed. She told me everything."

Henry straightened and leaned back. "Perhaps she told you what you wanted to hear. Perhaps she thought to ease your fears by finding a more plausible explanation."

"Lord Morford did not think so." There, she had played her ace card in this game of wits and strategy. While her face conveyed no emotion, inside she was jumping for joy.

"Lord Morford? What has he got to do with anything?"

"Lord Morford was with me at Highley Grange. Together we witnessed the strange occurrences. Together we discovered the servants hiding in the secret room, questioned their motive for behaving so appallingly." It was only a slight exaggeration.

Struggling to form a word, Henry stared at her blankly.

The seconds ticked.

During the awkward silence, her mind raced through their conversation. If Henry did not want to sell the house to pay a debt, what reason could he have for wanting her out? Unless hosting lewd parties was in the blood and he thought to carry on the tradition.

It was time to stop playing games.

Isabella squared her shoulders. "As you seem unable to provide me with an explanation, let me make my position clear." Her sharp tone conveyed the true nature of her emotions. "I will tell everyone willing to listen that you plotted to have me removed from the house so you could use it for sordid little parties. Those who know of your father's reputation will believe it to be true. Lord Morford will tell everyone how you terrorised an innocent woman purely out of a need to satisfy your debauched cravings."

The muscle in his cheek twitched. "That is simply not true."

She smirked. "Gossips do not care for the truth. Indeed, being made aware of the desperate lengths you would go to in order to get your way, there will be some who will wonder if you killed your father."

Her remark was equivalent to a sharp slap to the face or a hard punch to the gut. Rather than appear offended she saw anguish flash briefly in his dull green eyes.

"What sort of man do you take me for?"

"A man who will do anything to get his way," she whispered.

He raked his hand through his hair before giving a sigh of resignation. "If I am honest with you and tell you of my plans, do you swear you will tell no one?"

She owed Henry nothing. After everything he had done, she should tell him to go to the devil. But she was tired. If she had any hope of moving on with her life, she needed to put all this nonsense behind her.

"Whatever you tell me in confidence will not be repeated. Unlike some, I do have morals."

Henry nodded as though he deserved to feel the razor-sharp edge of her tongue. Cupping her elbow, he escorted her to the alcove further along the corridor where it was quieter. "Mrs. Forester is a dear friend. Of course, you know Mr. Forester is still of this world, although he is rarely seen in town."

"Yes," she said, despite assuming the woman was a widow.

"Mrs. Forester has a sister in Cambridge. Highley Grange would be the perfect place for us to … to meet on occasion."

It took a moment for her to absorb his words. "You mean to tell me your intention was to see me removed from my home so you could meet your mistress there?"

Good Lord. It beggared belief. The man had the morals of a guttersnipe.

"It was also out of interest for your welfare," he implored. "It is degrading to have to live in the place where one's husband …" He gave an odd wave. "You will be happy at Grangefields. I promise you."

Isabella clutched her throat for fear of throttling the man. "No, I won't, because I am not moving to Grangefields."

Henry appeared a little shocked. "But you said—"

"No. I have listened to you waffle on about your needs, yet not once have you apologised for the distress you have caused. Whilst your father may have been depraved in his appetites at least he was honest." She could feel her anger breaching the dam she had built to hold her emotions at bay. "Your behaviour is despicable."

All traces of emotion were wiped from his face, replaced with his mask of indifference. "If you refuse to concede to my wishes, know that I can make your life at Highley Grange uncomfortable."

"No, you can't." She would rather live in a tiny one-roomed cottage than be beholden to such a loathsome gentleman. "And just to clarify, I will not be living at Highley Grange, either."

He gave an arrogant smirk. Hope flashed in his eyes. "And where will you go?"

"I'm afraid I refuse to discuss my private affairs with you or with anyone," she said, hitting him with his own words.

The door to the card room creaked open. Matthew Chandler exited. He paused outside, leant back against the wall and sucked in a ragged breath. With a vigorous shake of the head, he straightened. Locking gazes with her, he inclined his head as he made his way back to the ballroom.

"There goes another pathetic fool," Henry said with a sneer.

His comment irritated her. "I do ask one thing. During the hauntings, items of value have gone missing from the house. I want them returned to me. Else I shall be forced to follow your unprincipled example and break a confidence. I may write to Mr. Forester to convey my concerns for my stepson, who has been lured to sin."

Fear flickered in his eyes. "I do not know anything about any missing items."

"I do not care about the silver pin pot, the crystal vase or the candlestick, to name but a few items. They belonged to your father, now to you. But I would like my ruby brooch. Perhaps your man, Mr. Blackwood, may be able to enlighten you as to its whereabouts."

"I have already told you. I made no instruction to remove valuable items."

"But you did instruct the servants to frighten me?"

He dragged his hand through his hair. "Yes. Yes. But I shall speak to Mr. Blackwood about your missing brooch. Perhaps it was part of the charade."

Had she been a spiteful, vindictive woman, she would have informed every guest at the Holbrooks' townhouse of Lord

Fernall's illicit affair with Mrs. Forester. Indeed, she would have found more than one biblical quote to support her need to repay him for all pain inflicted.

"Part of the charade?" she repeated, scrunching her nose in disgust. "Was your father's death also part of the charade? And what of Andrew, the previous Lord Morford? I know he spoke to you regarding Samuel's accident."

"Then you must also know that I have witnesses who can place me in Bath on the night my father died. You, on the other hand, were present in the house."

"Do you truly believe I killed your father?"

He paused. "No. I believe you were too indifferent to care."

"Those are probably the only honest words to fall from your lips. But I am done arguing with you. I shall return to Highley Grange and remove my personal belongings. When you discover what has happened to my brooch, you may return it to me at the house in Brook Street." Even if she had to take some form of paid work to pay the rent, she would not be beholden to Henry. "In fact, you may tell me where I can find Mr. Blackwood so I can ask him myself."

Henry shrugged. "He has lodgings on Gerrard Street above the drapers but he has been rather elusive of late."

"Elusive?"

"He disappears for a few hours most days, moves about from place to place. It is the reason he works so late into the evening."

She suspected the reason Mr. Blackwood was still in Henry's employ stemmed from his ability to organise a haunting. "I expect his talents far outweigh his lazy approach to his duties."

Henry ignored her comment. "Consider what I said about residing at Grangefields. A few weeks in town might make you change your mind."

She inclined her head, moved past him. "Oh, before I leave, let me wish you and Mrs. Forester much joy during your frequent stays at the Grange. I pray the house truly is haunted and that your nights there will not be as pleasurable as you hope or imagine."

Without another word she turned and strode down the corridor towards the ballroom. In leaving Highley Grange, she would be removing one of the shackles that bound her to Henry. It felt quite liberating. The gentleman could not be trusted, although she had never thought him guilty of murder.

Mr. Blackwood, on the hand, certainly had the opportunity.

He had worked for Samuel for three years or more though she had only met him on a handful of occasions. Judging by the faint hint of suspicion in Henry's eyes, Mr. Blackwood might be guilty of more than deception.

Theft might have been his motive for murder.

# CHAPTER 17

Tristan waited for Isabella out on the terrace. Three times he had circled the ballroom searching for her. Pushing and jostling with other guests had led to more than a few cross words. He rubbed the back of his neck to ease the mounting tension. Five more minutes and then he would rip the house apart.

Hearing the sound of footsteps, he glanced up to see Matthew Chandler approaching. "How did you fare?" Tristan asked, although judging by the solemn look on his friend's face the answer was not very well.

"Oh, you know," Chandler said with a shrug, "I lost more than I intended."

Chandler was a man who accepted life's challenges with good grace, although Tristan believed his friend's indifference was merely a mask. "Should I race around to your house and hide the pistols?"

"It would take more than a gambling debt to finish me." Chandler brushed his hand through his hair. "But I am not thinking clearly at the present moment. I sense something is amiss."

"Amiss? Are you referring to the card game?"

He shrugged. "Perhaps. We shall see if the outcome is as I suspect." With a quick glance back over his shoulder, he added, "Should I discover there is foul play afoot then those gentlemen will take it in turns to stare down the barrel of my pistol."

Tristan knew Chandler well enough to know he would not do anything rash. "I shall call on you tomorrow. When you have had a chance to reflect on the night's events, you can explain your suspicions to me then."

"Presuming I have not fled the country," Chandler said in jest.

"Tell me it is not so dire a situation as that."

"No. But I shall have to increase membership to my private gatherings."

Tristan breathed a sigh. "With your scandalous reputation, I do not think that will pose too much of a problem."

They were disturbed by a footman carrying a silver tray.

"My lord," he said, bowing to both gentlemen but focusing his attention on Tristan. "I have been instructed to deliver a missive."

Tristan glanced at the folded paper on the tray with some curiosity. "Thank you." The footman waited while Tristan scanned the short message. "You may leave us. There will be no reply."

The footman offered a graceful bow and made a discreet exit.

"There is somewhere I need to be," Tristan said, smiling to himself at the thought of meeting Isabella by the fountain. "But I'm a little reluctant to leave you here alone."

Chandler chuckled. "We are not at school now. I shall manage perfectly well. Besides, I need to find a way to distract my mind."

"Am I to assume you mean a distraction of the feminine persuasion?"

"What else is there?" He gestured to the folded paper in Tristan's hand. "By all accounts, I am not the only one eager to partake in an amorous liaison. I suggest you make haste before your lady grows tired of waiting."

Tristan cast him a huge grin. "I hope your night proves rewarding. I shall call on you tomorrow."

"Make sure it is after two. I hope to be thoroughly spent and exhausted and doubt I shall see my bed before dawn."

They parted ways.

Chandler returned to the ballroom whilst Tristan hurried down the steps and into the garden. Having never been to the Holbrooks' house before, he had no idea where to find the damn fountain. It was dark. A grey mist still hung in the air. He imagined it would be in a prominent place. Yet after a few minutes searching behind various hedges, he located it tucked away in a discreet corner.

As he approached, he could hear a soft whimpering sound. Had it not been for Isabella's note he would have made a hasty retreat. But he felt a sudden tightness in his abdomen that told him something was wrong.

"Isabella?" he whispered. If Henry Fernall had harmed her in any way, he would call the gentleman out and to hell with the consequences. "Isabella."

He heard the lady's sob before she appeared from a shadowed corner of the hedgerow.

"Miss Smythe?" He blinked rapidly in a bid to recover from his initial surprise. "What on earth are you doing out here?" He glanced past her shoulder, sagged with relief when he realised she was alone.

The lady stepped forward, squinted as she peered at him in the darkness. "Lord ... Lord Morford?" She took another hesitant step towards him. "Oh, my lord, I am so relieved it is you."

Tristan scanned the long golden curls hanging loosely from her coiffure. He questioned why she was clutching the shoulder

163

of her ivory gown until he realised it was torn, the left half of the bodice ripped, hanging down.

"What has happened to your gown?"

Miss Smythe grasped his arm, forgetting that it was the same hand she had used to cover her modesty, and consequently revealing more of her person than expected. "Your mother told Miss Hamilton that she wanted to speak to me privately out on the terrace."

His mother?

"I decided to avoid her, as I know how determined she can be." Miss Smythe gave a weary sigh. "But then I thought it was better to speak to her, to make my intentions clear."

"And what did she say?" Tristan was still struggling with the notion that his mother insisted on using manipulative tricks to get her way.

"That is what is so strange." Miss Smythe sniffed. "I waited, but she never came. Then I thought I saw her waving at me from the bottom of the garden and so I followed her out here."

"Did you speak to her?" When he returned to Bedford Square, he would arrange for his mother's trunks to be packed and inform the coachman not to stop until he reached Ripon.

"No. I looked for her but—" She broke off and gave an odd growl of frustration. "Perhaps I am losing my mind. None of it makes any sense."

Tristan considered the lady's dishevelled state. "You must try to remain calm. How did your gown come to be in such a state of disrepair?"

Miss Smythe sucked in a breath as she glanced at the ripped bodice. "This is going to sound ridiculous, I know, but as I approached the fountain a figure pounced from behind the shrubbery. He grabbed the sleeve of my gown and tugged at it until I heard the material tear. And then he simply ran off into the night."

Tristan rubbed his aching temple. He had never encountered

so many tangled mysteries, not even whilst working for the Crown. "Did you recognise this man who attacked you?"

She shook her head vigorously, rather too vigorously considering the deplorable state of her attire. "It was too dark, and he approached me from behind. I know he wore shoes with golden buckles. He smelt of bergamot and some strange exotic spice."

Tristan gestured to the exposed undergarment beneath the bodice of her gown and then focused his gaze on her face. "That could be any one of a hundred gentlemen in the ballroom this evening."

She put her hand to her chest. "Oh, what am I to do? Should anyone see my like this I shall be ruined beyond redemption."

Tristan suspected that was his mother's intention.

"Just give me a moment to think." He turned away, put his fingers to his forehead and rubbed in the hope something would spring to mind amidst the confusion. "I shall go and find Lady Fernall," he said, turning back to face a distraught Miss Smythe. "You may borrow her cape. She will escort you to her carriage and see you safely home."

For a moment he thought the lady might fall to her knees, such was the depth of gratitude expressed on her pretty face. "I cannot thank you enough, my lord. You must know, had I not been meeting your mother I would not have dared to venture out here alone." Miss Smythe's bottom lip trembled. She hit the skirt of her gown in a sudden fit of temper. "Oh, I have often mocked those for their naivety, and now I am the most foolish of them all."

"Calm yourself, Miss Smythe." Tristan waved his hands in the hope it would help. "Now, you must hide in the shrubbery and wait for Lady Fernall to arrive. She will call out to you, so—"

The sound of a gentleman's foul curse punctured the already tense air. Tristan scanned the topiary hedge, the frantic shuffling of his feet mirroring the wild flitting of his eyes.

Miss Smythe stepped closer, put her hand on his arm. "Oh, we are too late, my lord."

With that, Matthew Chandler appeared from the archway in the opposite side of the hedgerow. He stopped before them, put his hands on his knees as he struggled to catch his breath.

"This is not what it looks like," Tristan said, though when it came to Chandler, he had no need to defend his actions.

"I know," Chandler said straightening. "That's why I am here." His gaze scanned Miss Smythe's petite form, falling to the exposed curve of her soft bosom. He blinked and shook his head. "You have approximately two minutes before the group of matrons ambling around the perimeter of the garden find you here."

"Bloody hell!" Tristan pushed his hand through his hair. His mother knew how to execute a plan to perfection. "Tell me this is some sort of joke." He turned to the lady at his side. "Forgive me, Miss Smythe. I did not mean to curse."

Miss Smythe clutched her throat. "What are we to do?"

"I would have suggested making an exit through the arch," Chandler said, "but numerous guests are wandering about at the top of the garden."

Panic flared.

Tristan's blood pumped through his body at far too rapid a rate. To be caught alone in a secluded part of the garden was enough to force a betrothal. One look at Miss Smythe and he would be forever known as the scandalous rogue who ravished an innocent maiden on the grass next to the Holbrooks' fountain.

Damn it all!

Despite the depth of his feelings for Isabella, he could not leave Miss Smythe to the wolves.

He threw his hands up in despair. "There is nothing to be done. I fear my mother knows how to execute a deception with military precision. We are but pathetic pawns in her game."

"I must say I was surprised to see your mother in attendance," Chandler said. "When I saw Lady Fernall scouring the ballroom looking for you, I knew something was amiss."

The faint sound of feminine chatter drifted through the night air.

Hell and damnation!

Tristan turned to Chandler. His head felt heavy, his mind nothing but a mushy mass. "Leave us. It would not serve Miss Smythe well if she were caught alone with two gentlemen."

Despite the fraught situation, Chandler still seemed remarkably calm. "But what will you do?"

Tristan shrugged. "I don't have the remotest idea. Pray that the matrons decide to turn back. Hope for a miracle. But knowing my mother, I assume we will have no choice but to wed."

"Oh, this is dreadful," Miss Smythe cried. She covered her face with her hands.

Chandler came to stand in front of Miss Smythe. He took hold of her hands and brought them down to her side. "Do you want to marry Lord Morford?" he said in his usual rich drawl as he stared into her eyes.

Miss Smythe sucked in a breath, visibly swallowed as she held his gaze. "No," she said, shaking her head too many times to count. "I do not want to marry Lord Morford. But what else can I do?"

Chandler's gaze dropped to the lady's bosom. A smile touched the corners of his mouth as he brought her hands to his lips. "Would you like to marry me?" he said as he brushed his mouth against her gloves.

"What the blazes?" Tristan whispered. "We are trying to salvage something of the lady's reputation, not ruin it completely."

Miss Smythe pursed her lips as her gaze travelled over the breadth of Chandler's chest. "Is ... is that an offer, sir?"

Chandler nodded. "It is."

"I can't let you do that," Tristan objected.

Chandler shrugged. "It is not your decision to make."

"I am told the fountain is somewhere here." The chatter from behind the trimmed topiary sounded much clearer now.

Tristan's heart thumped hard against his ribs. "You must decide what you want to do, Miss Smythe," he said, struggling to keep his voice low.

Miss Smythe glanced down at her silk slippers before lifting her head. "Are you able to provide for me, sir?"

"Have no fear," Chandler replied with an arrogant smirk. "I shall ensure all your needs are met."

A blush touched Miss Smythe's cheeks, and she inclined her head. "Then I accept."

Good Lord!

Had there been time, he would have protested. Not because he believed Matthew would make an appalling husband—on the contrary, his friend had many honourable qualities—but because they were so unsuited.

"You need to leave, Tristan. You need to leave now." Chandler gestured to the archway. "Call on me tomorrow."

Tristan nodded, though his mind struggled to make sense of the night's events. He hovered at the arched exit, turned to see Chandler take Miss Smythe in his arms.

"Now, when people are gossiping about our tryst," Chandler said, staring into the lady's eyes, "what is it you want them to say about us? Is this to be a ravishing? Do you wish to be portrayed as a naive woman who was lured into a trap by a rogue?"

Miss Smythe shook her head. "I do not want anyone to think I am so foolish. No," she added with some determination. "If I have a choice, I would like people to say it is a lo-love match. I want people to think we were so consumed with passion we simply lost our heads."

Good God. Did the lady know what she was asking?

Chandler's mouth curled up into a sinful smile. "That is what I hoped you would say. From the moment we are discovered that is how we will play this game. You have my word, as a gentleman, that I will ask for your hand. But for now, I am going to kiss you with such vigour and passion that I believe we truly will lose our heads."

Tristan stepped back into the shadows. Miss Smythe's sweet sigh and Matthew Chandler's mumbled curse of appreciation were drowned out by a series of high-pitched feminine shrieks.

# CHAPTER 18

"*A*ll in all, it has been a rather eventful evening." Isabella sat back in the leather seat as her carriage rattled along the cobbles on its way to Brook Street. She considered the deep furrows between Tristan's brows. "What troubles you the most? Is it your mother's utter lack of morals or the prospect that Miss Smythe will have no option but to marry Mr. Chandler?"

Tristan folded his arms across his chest and leant back. "I don't suppose for a moment my mother considered what would happen to Miss Smythe should there be a fault with her plan."

Isabella sighed. "What would you have done had Mr. Chandler not appeared from the shrubbery to save the day?" She knew the answer. Tristan would not have let an innocent woman suffer. It was one of the many reasons she loved him.

He caught her gaze but struggled to hold it. "I ... I would have been forced to act in the only honourable way."

She smiled, despite the stabbing pains in her heart as she imagined him marrying another. "I would not have expected anything less."

For the first time since reuniting with him in the Holbrooks' ballroom, a smile touched the corners of his mouth. "I've always tried to see the best in every situation. To focus on the negative aspects causes nothing but misery. What Chandler did for me tonight, well, there are no words to express my gratitude."

It seemed Mr. Chandler did have some redeeming qualities.

"After the sacrifice he has made to save Miss Smythe, I'm confident there is good in him. If the lady is willing, she may find there is a respectable gentleman buried beneath the bravado and arrogant façade."

Tristan shook his head. "I'm just not sure she has the strength of will to deal with him. The lady likes embroidery and sewing, whilst Chandler is responsible for tearing the material of many ladies' undergarments."

Mr. Chandler oozed charisma. A man with his voracious appetite would know how to please his wife. "The quiet ones are often the most surprising. You would be amazed how far a woman will go to protect what is hers."

He raised a quizzical brow. "And how far would you go to protect what we have?"

In an instant, the air about them pulsed with a sensual intensity.

She smiled. It was a covert way of asking what he meant to her. "There is nothing I would not do for you." She met his heated gaze, conveyed a lifetime's worth of love.

He seemed pleased with her answer, yet she knew all he wanted was to hear a more definitive declaration.

"Then know that I feel the same." There was a moment of silence before Tristan rubbed his dimpled chin and said, "One thing does disturb me about the whole thing."

"Are you still referring to the incident with Miss Smythe," Isabella said with a mocking snigger, "or to the hauntings, the suspicious deaths or your mother's plot to ruin our lives?"

"It all sounds so unbelievable when you say it like that. No, I was referring to the incident with Miss Smythe. When I found her near the fountain, her gown was torn at the shoulder. She said a gentleman accosted her." He removed his hat, placed it on the seat next to him and scratched his head. "There is no doubt my mother played a part, but who ripped Miss Smythe's gown?"

"Whoever he was, I suspect your mother paid him handsomely in return for his assistance." Indeed, there were a handful of men who had gambled away their souls on the turn of a card. "With some persuasion, I am sure your mother will reveal his identity. And no doubt Mr. Chandler will have something to say about the matter."

Tristan cradled his head in his hands. "Damn it all. I cannot help but feel responsible for what happened. What if it ends in disaster? Two lives ruined, and for what?"

It was not like him to have such a cynical approach.

"And what if it is the making of them?" she said with an air of confidence. "From your earlier account, they seemed perfectly content when you left the garden." Yes, Mr. Chandler was reckless, but she was convinced Miss Smythe would prove to be a calming influence. "We will give them our support and help in any way we can."

"We?" His eyes twinkled with the boyish charm she so loved. "Does that mean you intend to see more of me?"

His words roused various lascivious images. The sudden pulsing between her thighs made her shiver. "I should like to see a lot more of you," she said, knowing he would hear the hitch of desire in her voice.

"That can easily be arranged."

Isabella shook her head. "You really are incorrigible."

"Isn't that one of the things you love about me?"

"Perhaps."

Tristan chuckled. "In my haste to tell you of Chandler's predicament, I did not ask how you fared with Henry Fernall."

Isabella tutted and waved her hand to show her frustration. "The gentleman is a selfish prig. He wanted me out of Highley Grange so he could use the house to entertain his mistress."

Tristan's expression darkened. "You do realise I could call him out for what he has done to you."

Panic flared. "Oh, he is simply not worth bothering about." Good Lord. She could not cope with the thought she might lose Tristan again. "Promise me you won't do anything rash. One way or another bad fortune will find him."

Tristan did not seem appeased. "At the very least I will have a few things to say on the matter, and I do not expect it to be pleasant."

A warm feeling filled her chest. To feel cherished, loved and protected was all she had ever wanted. "Henry did say something of interest. It so happens that Mr. Blackwood has been acting rather strangely of late," she said to distract his mind from thoughts of fights and duels. "He disappears for hours when he should be working."

Tristan shrugged. "A man who would orchestrate the terrible things that happened to you undoubtedly has loose morals."

"But Henry said Mr. Blackwood flits from place to place."

"It is feasible that he would take a short-term tenancy when in town or use a guest house. That way he is not liable for rent when staying at Highley Grange."

Tristan's points were logical. Yet she could not shake the feeling that Mr. Blackwood had something to hide. "When I questioned Henry about the missing items he denied any involvement."

"Please tell me you did not expect him to confess." Tristan snorted. "He would not want it known he had arranged for someone to steal items from his own home. People are suspicious by nature and would suspect fraudulent activity."

"What need has Henry for a silver pin pot and candlestick? He could buy a hundred if he so wished." Indeed, he had ample funds to purchase a house in Cambridge to entertain his mistress. Then again, her stepson was nothing if not frugal. "No. I am convinced Mr. Blackwood has stolen the items. Of course,

173

Henry cannot say anything to him. Not unless he wants to risk others discovering the deplorable methods he used to get rid of me."

"I suppose a haunted house provides the perfect opportunity to pilfer, for one can then blame it on the ghost."

She chuckled. But a few days ago, she would have trembled in fear at the mere mention of haunted houses. "I don't care about Henry's missing possessions. But I care that Mr. Blackwood has taken my brooch. It belonged to my mother." And she cared that Mr. Blackwood had played her for a fool. A sudden thought entered her head, and she gasped. "Do you think Mr. Blackwood stole from Samuel whilst working at Highley Grange?"

A debauched party would provide a perfect opportunity to steal from guests too inebriated to remember where they had put their snuffbox.

"It is possible."

She attempted to gauge what he was thinking. "But you are not convinced that is the case?"

"I did not say that. It is just impossible to prove."

It was easy to prove if they found Mr. Blackwood in possession of stolen goods.

"I do know where we might find the scoundrel," Isabella said with a hint of intrigue. "Mr. Blackwood has taken lodgings on Gerrard Street, above the drapers."

Tristan leant forward. "Are you suggesting we pay the gentleman a visit?" There was a wild glint in his eye that forced her to question the sense of such a plan. "I must say I am rather impatient to hear him try to defend his actions."

It was perhaps unwise to visit the home of a man who could have committed murder to protect his secret.

"I am confident we will not be in any danger." She kept her tone even so as not to reveal her fear. There was every chance

Tristan would insist on taking her home to Brook Street before heading off in search of Mr. Blackwood.

Tristan cleared his throat. "Perhaps you should wait—"

"No."

He raised a brow. "I'll not put you at risk. We do not know enough about the gentleman to make an informed decision."

Isabella raised her chin. "We go together, or we do not go at all."

"When I have dropped you at Brook Street, there is nothing stopping me from asking your coachman to take a detour on my way home."

"But it is a mile in the opposite direction." She moistened her lips, cast him her most sensual smile. "Besides, are you not staying the night with me in Brook Street? If you leave, I may be asleep by the time you return. There is every possibility the servants will fail to hear you knocking."

Inhaling deeply, he sat back in the seat and folded his arms across his chest. "Good God, woman, you certainly know how to get your own way."

The carriage rumbled to a halt on the corner of Gerrard and Wardour Street. The time was fast approaching midnight. There were but a few gentlemen ambling home, their inability to walk in a straight line proof of an evening spent in pursuit of pleasure.

Tristan stepped down to the pavement. "Wait further along the street," he called up to Dawes perched atop his box seat. "Wait near the turning into Gerrard Place."

"Yes, my lord."

He held out his hand to Isabella, savoured the frisson of awareness that always accompanied any physical contact.

"There is every chance Mr. Blackwood will not be at home,"

Isabella said as she stepped down to join him on the pavement. "For all we know he has returned to Highley Grange. As I said, he does seem rather keen to avoid me, and our paths rarely cross."

Tristan tucked her hand into the crook of his arm. They watched the carriage rattle away at a slow pace and disappear into the veil of mist. "Should that be the case, I suggest we make the journey to Hoddesdon tonight. We could catch him unawares, give him less of an opportunity to flee."

"I agree. I am rather keen to find some closure," she said with a sad sigh as she scanned the row of houses to their right. "I doubt we will ever know if Andrew's death was an accident or not. But at least we will know what part Mr. Blackwood played in it all."

They passed the tea shop, milliners and piano-forte maker before stopping outside the drapers. Peering in through the small square windowpanes, Tristan could see the rolls of material displayed behind the counter. He stepped back and surveyed the windows on the two upper floors. All was dark. There was not even a faint flicker of candlelight.

Tristan glanced at the weathered black door to the left, which no doubt provided access to the rooms above. "The best we can do is knock on the first door we come to and hope they have heard of Mr. Blackwood."

"One look at our attire and they will know we have not come to rob them."

Tristan opened the door. It led into a narrow hallway, and they climbed the stone stairs to the first floor. "Will you recognise Mr. Blackwood when you see him?"

"I have met him a handful of times over the years, but it has been at least three months since our paths have crossed at Highley Grange."

In itself, that was suspicious. Or perhaps the man had stolen Isabella's brooch and knew he would struggle to look her in the eye without revealing his guilt.

There were two doors on the first-floor landing. They knocked on the one nearest to the stairs, heard groans and grumbles emanating from within when they knocked for the third time.

"What have I told you drunkards about—" The woman stopped abruptly. She opened the door fully and met their gaze. With a quick glance at the quality of Isabella's vibrant gown, her filthy scowl became a beaming smile, despite the absence of a front tooth. "What can I do for you fine people at this very late hour?"

Isabella placed her hand on his arm, a gesture to inform him of her desire to address the woman. "We are looking for someone," she said. "A Mr. Blackwood. We were told he lives here."

The woman narrowed her gaze and scratched the greying hair at her temple. "A Mr. Blackwood you say? Does he have thick dark eyebrows that meet in the middle?"

"I would not say they were entirely thick, but they do meet just above the bridge of his nose."

"Does he have a large mole on his cheek?"

"Yes, I believe so," Isabella said with a sigh.

The woman rubbed her chin as she glanced up at the ceiling. "Does he have—"

"Good heavens," Tristan interrupted. "Can you just tell us if you know of him or not."

"He … he did live here, but now he's moved."

"When?" Tristan stepped closer. "Do you know where we might find him?"

"You're not the first to come here looking for him. I could tell by Blackwood's shifty stare he was up to no good." With a mischievous glint in her eye, the woman said, "It can get mighty cold at night." She took the ends of her shawl, wrapped them across her chest and shivered. "It doesn't help having the door open all this time."

Isabella nudged him.

He raised a brow in enquiry and through a series of animated facial expressions revealed he did not have so much as a coin on his person.

The woman raised her chin as she was obviously well-versed when it came to silent communication. "You know, it's not just woollen gloves what keeps your hands warm."

It did not take a genius to decipherer her meaning.

Isabella held her hand out. "What about these gloves? Do you think they will help keep the cold at bay? You may have them if you can tell us where we might find Mr. Blackwood."

Clasping her hands to her chest, the woman gasped. "Oh, how kind of you, madam, to think of an old woman in her hour of need."

Tugging the gloves at the ends of the fingers, Isabella pulled them off. She clutched them in her hand. "Mr. Blackwood's address and they are yours."

"Church Street."

Isabella offered the woman her silk gloves. "And the number."

"It's behind the modiste. Number twelve, on the ground floor. I do some sewing for her when she's running behind. That's how I know he's moved there."

Tristan put his hand out to prevent Isabella from delivering the prize. "Before we go, you mentioned someone else was curious to know of Mr. Blackwood's whereabouts. Do you recall this person's name?" Call it simple curiosity. Call it a need to be thorough in their investigation. "Did you tell them where to find the gentleman?"

The woman's rough fingers hovered in the air as she gripped the tip of the gloves. "He never gave his name. Neither did he offer any reward for keeping me standing at the door."

Tristan lowered his hand, and the woman greedily claimed her reward.

"Pleasure doing business. Please call again." With that, she closed the door to leave them standing in the hallway.

Isabella turned to him. "Well, I cannot say I have ever heard of Church Street."

"It is but a five-minute walk from here. We will instruct Dawes to wait in Wardour Street and then see if we can find the elusive Mr. Blackwood."

"Let us hope I do not have to use all my garments to barter for information."

Tristan cast a wicked grin. "Oh, I don't know. The idea has some appeal."

## CHAPTER 19

*T*he lodgings on Church Street were similar to those on Gerrard Street, but the entrance to the upper floors was via a dingy passageway between two buildings.

As with any place that offered protection from the harsh elements, what appeared to be a mound of clothes piled up against the wall was indeed a man sheltering beneath an oversize coat. Isabella covered the lower part of her face with her hand. Tristan imagined that the sudden stench of stale urine proved to be too overpowering for her. With no choice but to ignore the poor man's plea for a spare coin, they entered the building through the door in the alley. Unlike the previous premises, there was accommodation on the ground floor.

Tristan stepped forward and raised his hand to knock the paint-chipped door. "Let us hope the old woman told the truth and did not deceive us into giving her your best gloves. If you have to give away your slippers as a bribe for information, I am more than happy to carry you."

Isabella raised a brow. "We will lose your cravat before we lose anything else of mine."

He chuckled in the hope his amusement would help to ease

her anxiety. After all, Mr. Blackwood had engaged in criminal activity; Tristan knew many thieves who had progressed to murder.

Dismissing a faint hint of apprehension, he thumped the door with the side of his clenched fist. As expected, no one answered.

"It is ridiculously late," Isabella said moving to his side to assist him by rapping the crude brass knocker three times. "Perhaps he is tucked up in his bed."

Or perhaps the man was out fencing stolen goods.

The sound of shuffling on the other side of the door caught Tristan's attention. Unless rats were scurrying about the house, someone was listening to their every word.

Tristan put his mouth to the gap between the frame and the door. "Mr. Blackwood," he whispered. "We know you are in there. Let us in else we will be forced to call the constable."

The noises inside grew progressively louder. There was a range of mumbled curses, the dull thud of a heavy object falling to the floor.

Was it Mr. Blackwood's intention to make it obvious he was at home?

"It sounds as though he is moving the furniture," Isabella said.

"Bloody hell!" Tristan grabbed Isabella's hand. "No doubt he is attempting to climb out of the window."

They raced out into the dark alley, ignored the foul scent hanging in the air. They turned left and followed the cobbled path to a small courtyard at the rear of the building. A man, whom Tristan presumed to be Mr. Blackwood, sat astride the window ledge. With one leg on the ground and his head bent to navigate the low sash, the man was obviously trying to make his escape.

Tristan cleared his throat. "Ah, Mr. Blackwood, have you lost your key?"

The man craned his neck, gasped as his gaze fell to Isabella.

With wide eyes, Mr. Blackwood stared at her with a look of horror.

"Go away," he whispered. "Leave now before it is too late."

The words were far from threatening. In fact, if Tristan was not mistaken, Mr. Blackwood appeared utterly terrified.

"We are not leaving here until we have spoken to you." Tristan stepped forward. "Now, we can do that out here, or we can come inside. We can do that with or without a constable."

There was a tense moment of silence.

"We just want to talk to you," Isabella added, "and then we will leave you in peace."

"Peace?" Mr. Blackwood continued to mutter to himself. While the rest of his words were incoherent, his rapid, high-pitched tone revealed an element of distress. "I've not had a minute's peace for months. You … you had better come inside."

Isabella turned to Tristan and touched his arm. "If we leave he might not open the door."

She had a point. Whilst they were walking to the front door, Mr. Blackwood could easily escape through the window.

"I shall wait here," Tristan whispered. "I'll watch you walk down the alley until you are safely inside. Then I shall climb through the window."

Without a whimper or a murmur of protest, she nodded. The look of confidence flashing in her eyes made his chest swell with pride. She really was a remarkable woman.

Mr. Blackwood attempted to drag his leg through the window, but he stumbled back, until naught but the sole of his shoe was visible.

Tristan suppressed a snigger. "Once you have found your feet, you are to open the door for Lady Fernall. I shall enter via the window."

"It doesn't seem as though I have a choice," Blackwood groaned.

Tristan watched Isabella until she entered the building. After a minute or so, she appeared at the raised sash and assisted him as he climbed through into a small parlour.

Whilst Tristan brushed the cobwebs and dirt from his coat and breeches, Mr. Blackwood fiddled about with a tinderbox, lit the solitary candle and placed it on the mantelpiece. A musty smell lingered in the air but their host raced to the window, pulled down the sash and drew the dusty drapes.

The sparsely furnished room consisted of a small sofa and two chairs. The coverings were far more threadbare than the ones in Isabella's drawing room in Brook Street.

"You may as well sit." Mr. Blackwood gestured to the sofa. He waited for them both to take a seat before flopping into the chair nearest the hearth.

Tristan observed the man's demeanour. With his head hung low and his shoulders hunched, he did not appear to be capable of general everyday tasks, let alone theft and murder.

"Do you know why we are here?" Tristan stared at the sorry state of a man, waiting to catch his gaze.

"How did you know where to find me?" Mr. Blackwood looked up. A thick, dark line of hair ran the breadth of his forehead, giving the appearance of one eyebrow, not two.

"A charming lady in Gerrard Street told us where to come," Tristan informed him, his tone revealing a hint of pride in their investigative abilities.

Mr. Blackwood did not pass comment but lifted his chin in a look of resignation. "I suppose it was too much to expect I could go about unnoticed."

Isabella straightened. "Do you not have something to say to me, Mr. Blackwood? Do you not owe me an apology for arranging a rather terrifying welcoming party whenever I returned home to Highley Grange?"

The man's long slug of a brow twitched. "You know about the ghost then?"

Isabella scoffed. "The ghost? I think it is fair to say that Mrs.

Birch is still of this world. What I fail to understand is why you saw fit to carry out Lord Fernall's plans with such eagerness and commitment."

"It was for your own good, my lady." Blackwood did not even attempt to deny his involvement.

"My own good? Good heavens, I almost expired from fright."

Tristan patted her hands as they lay in her lap. "Lord Fernall has explained his reason for wanting the house vacated. Yet I do not see how, in any way, the outcome would prove satisfactory for Lady Fernall."

Mr. Blackwood pushed his hand through his hair and groaned. "While I am bound to act on my employer's request, that was not the only reason I arranged to frighten my lady away."

"Then tell us your reason." Tristan threw his hands up. "Good Lord, man, you owe the lady an explanation."

Mr. Blackwood shook his head. "What you don't know cannot hurt you."

Damnation. The man spoke in riddles.

"If you were so concerned for my welfare," Isabella began, "then tell me why you saw fit to steal from me. I know you took valuable items from Highley Grange. I know you have my brooch."

With another pitiful groan, Mr. Blackwood buried his head in his hands. "I don't have them anymore."

Tristan glanced at Isabella, noted the firm line of her jaw and knew she was struggling to suppress emotion. It was perhaps a little naive of her to assume the man had held on to something so precious.

"Are you telling me you do not have my brooch?" she said in choked voice. "Well, what you have done with it?"

"I've sold it, my lady." He looked up, his frantic gaze flitting about the room, struggling to settle on anything. "I had to find the funds to allow me to relocate. I couldn't take the risk of remaining in one place."

Isabella jumped to her feet. "You are not making any sense. Are you attempting to hide from your creditors? Have you gambled away a loan and now cannot repay? Heavens, will you not just explain yourself."

Tristan grasped her hand. He wanted to take her in his arms and make everything right. "Sit down, Lady Fernall. We must be calm if we are to discover the reasons behind Mr. Blackwood's actions."

There was no doubt now that the man was guilty of theft. His confession was enough to see him hang. But to threaten him would serve no purpose. There was more to the story than what appeared on the surface. Reassurance was now their best plan of action.

"We are here to help you, Mr. Blackwood." Tristan squeezed Isabella's hand as she sat down beside him. It, too, was a gesture of reassurance and trust. "But we must know the truth if we have any hope of solving our problems."

"I cannot say another word." Mr. Blackwood stared at Isabella. "It is for your protection, my lady."

"Then let us ask our questions," Tristan said, hoping to tease the information slowly from him. "And you may decide which ones you wish to answer." He paused whilst he thought how best to proceed.

"How long have you been stealing items from Highley Grange?" Isabella blurted before Tristan had a chance to speak. "I want a figure, nothing more."

"For … for just a few months. No longer than that. I swear."

The answer proved revealing.

Mr. Blackwood had been stealing items since Andrew's death, all to provide the money for him to hide away. A frosty chill shivered through him. Andrew may well have met his demise at the hands of another.

"How long have you been using untoward methods to frighten Lady Fernall?" Tristan asked, although his constant use of Isabella's married name was grating on him.

"For six months, maybe more. Since his lordship requested me to find a way to persuade Lady Fernall to leave."

"And you did not object because, in the first instance, you are in Lord Fernall's employ, and because you felt you were acting in the best interests of Lady Fernall," Tristan clarified.

Mr. Blackwood nodded. "That is correct."

"Were you responsible for frightening my husband during the few days before his death?"

She was obviously referring to Lord Fernall's accident with his horse and whatever had dragged him from his bed that night.

"No, my lady. No." Mr. Blackwood's bottom lip quivered when he answered. "I had nothing to do with that."

"But you know who did?" Tristan spoke quickly in the hope of catching the man off guard.

"Yes, but—no."

"I shall tell you my theory," Tristan said as his mind clambered to piece together the relevant bits of information. "For the last three months, you have avoided any contact with Lady Fernall. Whenever she is at Highley Grange, you are in town. You say your actions stem from a need to protect her. It stands to reason then that you know something that would place her in danger."

Mr. Blackwood stared at him with wide eyes. He tugged at his cravat as though the tight knot was restricting the flow of air. "I knew if I spent time in your company, my lady, I would say something I would later regret."

By nature of his nervous disposition Tristan believed Blackwood would also struggle to hide his guilt for his part in the mysterious hauntings.

"Why have you only shown concern for me these last three months when my husband has been dead for two years?" As soon as the words left Isabella's mouth she gasped. "Good Lord. You know what happened to Lord Morford the night he fell from his horse."

Tristan shuffled uncomfortably. A hard lump formed in his throat. "I am certain if we sat here long enough we would come up with the answers. You may as well explain yourself. As long as you do not divulge the culprit's name you have nothing to fear."

Blackwood's anxious gaze drifted back and forth between them.

"There is every chance we have been followed here," Isabella said. "Whilst we are running about blindly, the perpetrator will always be two steps ahead."

Mr. Blackwood dragged his hand down his face and sighed deeply. "I ... I know who killed Lord Fernall—"

"My husband was murdered?" Isabella shot to her feet. She clutched her throat and then dropped back onto the sofa. "I knew something was amiss. Was it his son, Henry Fernall?"

"No, my lady. But don't ask me for a name."

Tristan opened his mouth to speak, but it took a moment for him to form the words. "And did the same person murder my brother?"

Mr. Blackwood shook his head. "Your brother's accident happened just as they said. I was to ride with him back to London. But I was late and attempted to catch up with him near Hoddesdon."

Tristan dragged his hand down his face. Relief flowed through him. Nothing would bring his brother back but knowing his death was an accident was perhaps easier to bear.

"I had told him about the night Lord Fernall died," Mr. Blackwood continued. Now he had begun his story the words flowed freely. "I'd not wanted to tell a soul, but his lordship had a commanding way about him. He wanted me to go to London, to confront the gentleman responsible. But I avoided him, hid in the woods opposite the gates and watched him leave without me."

"Were you afraid to speak up?" Isabella asked, her tone soft, serene.

"I'm the only witness. I didn't want to reveal what I saw that night. But his lordship asked too many questions, prodding and probing until my mind was a jumbled mess."

Tristan suspected it would not take a great deal of effort to push the man to his limits.

"But something made you change your mind," Tristan said, "else you would not have attempted to follow my brother."

Mr. Blackwood shrugged. "I kept thinking, what if the scoundrel came back to Highley Grange? What if he thought to silence us all?"

"Did you not think to tell the current Lord Fernall what you saw?" Isabella said.

"At the time I had no proof. Besides, he is not an easy gentleman to talk to."

"And so you saw my brother fall from his horse?"

Blackwood nodded. "He was dead by the time I got to him. I thought to get help, but then I remembered the notebook." He hung his head. "I stole it from his saddle bag. When I heard the pounding of horse's hooves I made it away through the woods."

Isabella sighed. "And you have been running ever since."

Tristan's thoughts turned to Andrew's notes. "Do you still have my brother's book?"

Blackwood simply nodded.

"Why did you not think to bring it to me?"

"How could I when it was the only thing keeping me alive?" Blackwood implored.

Isabella sat forward. "The murderer knows you have the book?"

"I don't know what game Lord Morford was playing," Blackwood said, "but after his death, the gentleman came back to Highley Grange. He knew of my involvement, and I have used the notebook to blackmail him into staying away."

"A gentleman you say." Tristan had suspected a disgruntled guest was the likely candidate. "Has this gentleman not made some attempt to recover the book?"

"One night, I returned to the gatehouse to find the place had been ransacked. I have been mugged twice in the space of a month. It is why I must move, why I cannot be seen to follow a routine."

Everything was beginning to make more sense. "Is that why you wanted Lady Fernall to leave Highley Grange? Is it because you fear what the gentleman might do in his desperation to find the notebook?"

Blackwood nodded. "The gentleman is unstable I fear."

"And you are certain Lord Fernall did not simply trip and fall down the stairs?" Tristan had to ask the question. An innocent man would be just as determined to obtain slanderous material.

"Lord Fernall did not fall down the stairs." Blackwood's eyes grew large and wide. "The gentleman came up behind him and snapped his neck as though it was nothing more than a twig."

"Good Lord!" Tristan could not hide his shock. It took a cold, callous man to behave in such a vicious manner. "And you bore witness to the crime."

"I shouldn't have been in the house, but I'd taken Molly back to her room after … well … Mrs. Birch had locked the outer door leading to the servants' quarters and so we'd come through the main hall. On my way back, I heard the boards creaking on the landing and so hid at the bottom of the stairs."

"Did you not hear a conversation?" Isabella asked. "Did the gentleman not give a reason for killing my husband?"

"The gentleman crept up behind him. Lord Fernall was too slow to react. The gentleman caught his lordship before he hit the floor."

An eerie silence filled the room. Tristan presumed their minds were busy imagining the macabre scene.

Blackwood suddenly jumped in his chair. "I do remember the gentleman saying something, though I thought both things odd at the time."

"Yes?" they replied in unison, hanging on Blackwood's every word.

"As he twisted Lord Fernall's neck he said it was a little trick he had learnt in India. Then he threw Lord Fernall over his shoulder as though he was a sack of grain, carried him down the stairs and laid his body out on the floor. I hung back in the shadows, kept my hand across my mouth fearing he would hear me breathe."

"In India?" Tristan clarified.

"Yes," Blackwood replied. "And as he stood over the body, he said that the Devil reaps what he sows. Then he walked out of the front door."

"India," Tristan repeated.

"Does that mean something to you?" Isabella asked.

"It is just that I know someone who has recently returned from India," he said, rubbing his chin as the suspicious part of his mind grew more alert. "Perhaps it is simply a coincidence. After all, there must be many people who make such a journey."

"Samuel died two years ago. I doubt we are talking about the same person," Isabella said confidently.

She was right, of course. Besides, Mr. Fellows struck him as a man who lacked the strength to undo the knot in his cravat, let alone break a man's neck with his bare hands.

"How recently?" Blackwood said, chewing on his fingernail while he waited for a reply.

"Excuse me?"

"This person you are acquainted with, how recently did he return from India?"

"I'm not sure. A few months ago." Tristan shrugged. "I

WHAT YOU DESERVE

barely know the gentleman, but Mr. Fellows is far too affable—"
He stopped abruptly, aware of the look of horror on Mr. Blackwood's face. "What is it?"

Blackwood gulped. "Mr. Fellows? But that is the name of the
gentleman who murdered Lord Fernall."

# CHAPTER 20

"*D*o you think the plan will work?" Isabella rubbed the fine layer of mist from the carriage window with the tips of her fingers. She peered out into the dimly lit street, watched Mr. Blackwood's hazy form disappear through a cloud of fog. "What if Mr. Fellows is not at home?"

"Then Blackwood will leave a note for him to meet us in Green Park."

Doubt surfaced. "Mr. Blackwood scuttled away so quickly I do wonder if he will come back." Indeed, the man had been fraught with fear at the thought of confronting a murderer.

"Blackwood has nowhere else to go," Tristan said with an air of confidence as he lounged back against the squab. "He has neither the funds nor the resourcefulness to hide indefinitely. And I have a feeling it will only be a matter of time before Mr. Fellows discovers where he has hidden the notebook."

Isabella sat back in the seat. Staring out of the window only served to make the time pass more slowly. "I have seen Andrew examining his notes numerous times during his visits to Highley Grange, but he refused to disclose the information. I know he told me he was making enquiries, but I did not imagine he would discover anything of interest."

"I must say I am rather intrigued to read what he has written. Hopefully, there will be something we can use against Mr. Fellows."

"We can only pray." She dismissed the frisson of fear coursing through her. Should Mr. Fellows discover the extent of their involvement, they would be forever looking over their shoulders, too. "I shall be relieved to see an end to it all."

"Oh, I don't know," he said with an amused grin. "I rather enjoyed our ghost hunting in the dead of night. I particularly enjoyed kissing away your fears. And watching you writhe restlessly in your sleep, that delightful cotton nightdress getting wrapped around your shapely thighs."

His playful tone helped to ease her anxiety. "You observed me sleeping?"

"What else was I to do stuck in a rickety chair for hours?"

"But you said you could sleep anywhere."

Tristan grinned. "I can unless there is a tempting beauty lying but a few feet away, calling out to me during her whimsical dreams."

Panic flared. "What … what did I say?"

Tristan rubbed his chin as he stared thoughtfully at a point beyond her shoulder. "You said something about how pleased you were to have me home."

She narrowed her gaze. "Had I been talking about you I would have said something far more salacious, though I am pleased you found a modicum of pleasure whilst cramped in the chair." Her most memorable moment had occurred a little later. "I much preferred our early evening activities. Who would have thought that a waltz in a musty drawing room could be so stimulating?"

His heated gaze bored into her soul. "When we return to Brook Street, we will have to work on improving our line."

Desire unfurled. "How can one improve on perfection?"

"We could try a new dance. Something novel yet equally satisfying."

Had they been alone, she was confident they would not have waited another second to fall into each other's arms.

With the highly charged feeling of unsated desire in the air, they fell into a companionable silence, though she suspected they were both lost in amorous thoughts.

She could not help but stare at him. Tristan closed his eyes, his breathing slowing to a calm, relaxed rate. Mere days ago she thought they would never share a civil word. Now, they had indulged their deepest passions, shared their darkest desires. Joining with him had been the most precious, most fulfilling moment of her life.

The sudden creak of the carriage door as it flew open dragged her out of her reverie.

Mr. Blackwood clambered inside, his ragged breathing evidence he had run all the way back to the conveyance.

"Did you speak to him?" Tristan straightened, closed the door and thumped the roof to alert Dawes of their intention to leave.

The carriage lurched forward almost immediately.

"Quick, you must h-hurry," Mr. Blackwood stammered as he grabbed on to the edge of the seat to stop himself falling forward. "He cannot know we are together."

"You spoke to Mr. Fellows?" Tristan reiterated.

Mr. Blackwood nodded vigorously. "Yes. Yes. He has agreed to meet me near the D-Dead Man's Tree in Green Park."

"The Dead Man's Tree?" She had heard that the park was once a haunt for highwaymen, a place renowned for notorious duels. "That sounds rather ominous."

"Some refer to it as the Tree of Death," Tristan said. "It is a popular place for those who wish to end their lives ... prematurely."

Despite his tactful explanation, she recoiled as she imagined stumbling upon a stiff body swaying from a bough.

"There is something so sinister about excessive facial hair," Mr. Blackwood randomly said as he shivered visibly. "Mr. Fellows' bushy side-whiskers give him a menacing aura. I swear, had I the notebook in my possession he would have broken my neck on the doorstep."

Isabella stared at Mr. Blackwood sitting opposite. Had the man never glanced in the mirror? Did he not know his eyebrows were just as strange and forbidding?

Tristan cast Mr. Blackwood a sidelong glance. "Did you inform him you wished to make an exchange?"

"Yes. He promised two hundred pounds for the book. I told him … I told him I planned to move away, that I have a cousin in Lancashire and had no desire to return to the city. I told him I am tired of hiding in the shadows."

"Did he believe you?"

Mr. Blackwood shrugged.

Tristan removed his pocket watch and angled the face towards the window. "It is just past three. Did you tell him to meet you at five?"

"Yes, five as you suggested."

"Then you will need to tell us where you hid the notebook, Mr. Blackwood," Isabella said. She understood his need for secrecy but time was of the essence. "We must retrieve it if we are to meet Mr. Fellows."

It was Tristan who spoke. "Er, Mr. Blackwood has told me where he has hidden the book. I have already informed Dawes of our destination."

"Oh." No one had thought to mention it to her. "Is it far?"

"No. Just off Grosvenor Square."

It suddenly occurred to her that Tristan had not mentioned what he intended to do once at Green Park. "If the notebook contains the proof needed to substantiate the allegations against

Mr. Fellows, why do we need to meet him in the park? Surely it is best to go straight to the authorities."

Tristan shuffled in his seat. "We cannot trust the authorities to act quickly enough. With Mr. Blackwood being the only witness, Mr. Fellows could easily find a way to manipulate him. Equally, the book may prove to be useless. No. I'm afraid we need a confession."

She suspected he meant to say something far more sinister than *manipulate* but did not wish to frighten Mr. Blackwood any more than was necessary. "It will only be our word against his. If you don't mind me saying, it is all very speculative considering we do not know what is written in the notebook."

"We don't need to know," Tristan replied. "Fellows believes the book incriminates him. We will use it as a bargaining tool to force him to admit his crimes. And the word of two peers will help to bolster our cause."

"Two peers?"

The carriage rumbled to a halt before Tristan could answer. Isabella wiped the window and peered at the imposing townhouse. The tall Doric columns supporting the portico looked familiar, as did the brass door knocker in the shape of a lion's head.

"But this is Lord Fernall's house," she said, her high-pitched tone revealing her surprise.

"I … I have been overseeing the renovations to the upper rooms," Mr. Blackwood informed. "I thought it a perfect place to hide the notebook. Should anything untoward happen to me, then I hoped Lord Fernall might one day stumble upon it and discover what really happened to his father."

"I assume Lord Fernall knows nothing of this." She sat back to give Tristan the opportunity to open the door. "Are we to inform him of our intentions or are we to sneak through the servants' quarters in the hope we are not noticed?"

"We need Lord Fernall's help." Tristan opened the door and vaulted down to the pavement. He smiled as he offered her his hand. "I'm afraid we've no choice but to knock on the front door."

## CHAPTER 21

hey were shown into Lord Fernall's study. Saunders went to rouse his master who had returned home but an hour before.

"I thought the butler was about to slam the door in our faces," Tristan said, pulling out the chair for her to sit. "That was until you introduced yourself."

It was the first time she had ever been thankful for bearing the Fernall name. "I have been to this house many times, but I believe Saunders has only worked here for a little over a year."

Tristan paced back and forth in the space to the right of her chair as they waited for Lord Fernall. He grumbled and sighed whenever he removed his pocket watch and glanced at the face. Mr. Blackwood hovered to her left, his breathing far too laboured for a man standing motionless.

"There is a perfectly good clock on the mantelpiece," she said. Tristan's fidgeting was starting to make her anxious. It did not take much to unnerve Mr. Blackwood. Indeed, she noted beads of perspiration on his brow, noted him wincing as he pressed his fingers to his temple.

Tristan tucked the offending item back into his pocket.

"There is something about the ritual of checking one's watch that appears to accelerate time."

"It is all in the mind," she countered.

The clip of brisk footsteps echoing through the hall captured their attention. Lord Fernall entered. The gentleman had obviously dressed in a hurry and had not quite managed to force his arm through the sleeve of his coat.

"What is the meaning of calling at such a late hour?" Henry's irate gaze drifted over them as he fumbled with his attire. When his penetrating stare settled on Mr. Blackwood, a muttered curse fell from his lips. He turned to her. "Have I not already explained my reasons for acting as I did? There was no need to drag poor Mr. Blackwood from his bed."

With a sudden wave of rage, Tristan stepped forward. "I should beat you to a pulp for what you have done to Isabella. What sort of gentleman terrifies a woman in her home?"

Henry's face flamed berry red. "Not that I have to explain myself to you," he began, "but I believed I was acting in Lady Fernall's best interest."

"Nonsense." Tristan squared his shoulders. "You wanted to throw her out to make way for your mistress?"

Henry glanced at Mr. Blackwood. "This is hardly the place to discuss such matters. I did not drag myself out of bed for you to berate me for my failures." He turned to face her. "I thought we had come to an agreement."

She stood, purely because she refused to be spoken down to, even literally. "We are not here to discuss the ghostly goings-on at Highley Grange. We are here because we have proof that someone murdered your father, and we need your help to ensure justice is served."

Henry frowned until his brows practically overhung his lids. He took two steps back, shook his head numerous times as though that would help to solve the problem with his hearing.

"Murdered?" he repeated. "Is this some sort of joke? Is this your way of exacting your revenge for me wanting you to leave Highley Grange?"

"It is all true, my lord." Mr. Blackwood stepped forward, his hands clasped in front of him. "I witnessed the event. I saw the man who murdered your father."

"Wait a minute." Henry rubbed his temple. "You witnessed my father's death and yet did not think to mention it before?"

"There was no proof, nothing but my word. I didn't think anyone would believe me." Mr. Blackwood looked to his feet. "It was cowardly of me to remain silent. I know that now."

"I have always suspected foul play," Isabella said, lifting her chin. "But my opinion was partly based on the suspicious incidents occurring at the Grange."

Tristan cleared his throat. "In a bid to settle Lady Fernall's fears my brother conducted an investigation. He wrote everything down in a notebook which Mr. Blackwood retrieved upon my brother's death and which is now hidden somewhere in this house. The murderer wants it and has arranged to meet Mr. Blackwood in order to make a trade."

Henry's eyes grew large and wide as his curious gaze scanned the room. "You left the notebook here?" he snapped. "Good Lord. There is a criminal on the loose, and you left an incriminating piece of evidence in my house." Henry rubbed the back of his neck. Judging by the flash of fear in his eyes he appeared grateful his head was still firmly attached to his body. "And are you here to reclaim this book?"

Mr. Blackwood shuffled from one foot to the other. "It is hidden under the boards in what will be the new master chamber. We must take it with us."

"Then go and get it this instant." Henry's frantic hand movements revealed his impatience.

Mr. Blackwood scuttled from the room.

They waited in silence.

The tension in the air felt heavy and oppressive.

Henry paced back and forth in a military fashion, whilst Tristan's clenched jaw and disapproving stare conveyed an emotion that could best be described as menacing.

Mr. Blackwood's frantic steps could be heard racing through the hall, but he slowed to a walking pace as he entered the study. "Here ... here it is." He waved the small leather-bound book, first at Tristan and then at Henry, not knowing what to do. No doubt his loyalty to his employer would play a hand in forcing his decision.

"The notebook belongs to Lord Morford," Isabella said to bring clarity to the situation. "It is his by rights, regardless of where it has been kept."

The corners of Tristan's mouth curved up into a discreet grin as their gazes locked. His blue eyes sparkled with a vitality that stole her breath.

"Then give it to him," Henry snapped as he shooed Mr. Blackwood away. "I am tired and in need of my bed."

Tristan took the notebook. He ran his fingers over the brown leather, placed his palm flat on the cover as though it still contained the essence of his brother. With a shake of the head, he flipped the book open and scanned the pages, stopped periodically and traced various words with the tip of his finger.

She moved to his side, resisted the urge to touch his arm, to peer over his shoulder. Regardless of Andrew's failings, it must hurt to read the words, knowing he would never have another opportunity to hear his brother's voice.

"Is it what we suspected?" she asked softly. "Is there anything we can use to support Mr. Blackwood's statement?"

Tristan looked up at her. It was not pain she saw in his eyes but rather a glint of satisfaction that suggested Andrew had been thorough in his investigation. "We have the times and dates of passage for numerous trips to India. We have a list of all the gentlemen who attended Samuel Fernall's events at Highley Grange, one of whom is Mr. Fellows. We—"

"Mr. Fellows?" Henry interjected. "The gentleman with the extravagant side-whiskers?"

"Have you had dealings with the gentleman before?" Isabella asked. She could not imagine Henry participating in his father's debauched games.

Henry cleared his throat. "I know he attended various parties at the Grange. Upon my father's wishes, I threw him out when he became ... shall we say rather loud and uncooperative."

"Good Lord." Tristan sucked in a breath as he studied one particular page.

"What is it?" Isabella put her hand to her throat as she anticipated his reply.

Tristan glanced up at Henry, pursed his lips as confusion marred his brow. "Are you aware of any other children your father may have sired?"

Pulling himself up to his full height, Henry said, "I am the only heir."

"That does not answer the question." Tristan cocked a brow in mild reproof. "You either know, or you don't."

Henry's arrogant façade faltered. "I am aware he was unfaithful to my mother, that he had numerous illegitimate offspring dotted about here and there."

"I was not aware," Isabella said, feeling a little disgruntled. She was surprised. Samuel had never felt the need to hide the licentious part of his character.

Tristan handed her the notebook. "It makes for interesting reading."

With some hesitation, she flicked through the first few leaves. There were pages of times, dates, the names of ships travelling to Madras. Mr. Fellows had left for India mere days after Samuel's death, returned a month before Andrew met his demise. There were pages of names, some peers, some she recognised. Andrew had taken statements from those whose dissipated antics were well known.

To say Andrew had done a thorough job was an understatement.

She turned the page and read the first few lines of what appeared to be a witness statement. Indeed, the time, date and location were recorded. "There is a testimony from a servant who worked for Mrs. Fellows. How on earth did Andrew get the maid to speak?"

Tristan shrugged. "If you read on, you will see that the servant was tending to Mrs. Fellows just before she died. The nurse heard Mrs. Fellows tell her son that he was illegitimate."

Henry scoffed. "If you are about to say that Mr. Fellows is my father's son, then I already suspected as much."

"What?" Tristan and Isabella said in unison.

A folded piece of paper fell from the notebook onto the floor. Tristan picked it up.

"I overheard an argument about money," Henry informed in a matter-of-fact tone. "I assumed it was over a gambling debt. But no doubt Mr. Fellows sought financial compensation."

She turned to Tristan, who was busy scanning the paper. "Is it anything of interest?"

Tristan stared at her though she could not gauge his mood. "It is certainly interesting, but it does not pertain to the case."

"May I see it?" She held out her hand, sensed his slight hesitation.

"Certainly. I believe it belongs to you."

Isabella took the paper, peeled back the folds to find a sketch of a naked woman. Focusing on the woman's eyes, she knew the figure was drawn in her likeness.

Henry stifled a yawn. "If you have what you came for can I retire to my bed?"

Tristan sucked in a breath. "Are you not the least bit interested in catching the man who murdered your father?"

"Good Lord, no. It was only a matter of time before one of his dissipated guests finished him off."

Isabella was struggling to focus on the conversation. She did not care that Andrew had made the sketch. But she feared Tristan would question how his brother came to possess such insight.

"I need you to come with us," Tristan said. "Should Mr. Fellows elude us, he may come here. The man is dangerous and unpredictable. I would not be at all surprised to find that you and the delightful Mrs. Forester are the casualties of a horrific carriage accident. Then again, house fires are common and hide any evidence of foul play."

Henry gulped. "Why … why should Mr. Fellows care what I think?"

"You're a witness. You can attest to the argument, to the volatile nature of his relationship with your father. You had the notebook in your possession." Tristan raised a brow. "Just think how grateful Mrs. Forester will be when she learns you captured a criminal in order to protect her."

Henry appeared to ponder the comment. "What would I have to do?"

"Nothing. You just need to bear witness to the conversation. You may tell Mrs. Forester what you wish. I will not discredit your account."

There was a brief moment of silence.

"Very well." Henry inclined his head. "Give me a moment and I shall come with you."

While they waited for Henry to return, Isabella took the opportunity to speak to Tristan.

"I had no idea Andrew had made this sketch," she said, taking his arm and pulling him to the furthest corner of the study.

"You mean you did not pose for him?" There was not a trace of suspicion or anger in his tone.

"Of course not." She could not hide the panic in her voice. "Please tell me you did not think I would do such a thing?"

A smile touched his lips. "In the first instance, I trust your word. In the second, it is evident that my brother has never seen you naked." He moistened his lips as he stared at her mouth. "Your hips are far more curvaceous, your breasts are fuller, more—"

"Yes. Yes." She waved her hand in the air as relief coursed through her. "You do not have to go into detail."

He took her hand, threaded his fingers through hers. "I want you to do something for me." His tone revealed a slight apprehension.

"You know I would do anything you asked."

"I do not want you to come to Green Park. I want you to wait for me in Brook Street."

She swallowed down the sudden pain in her throat. "But why? I will not be a burden."

His eyes grew bright, filled with affection. "You could never be a burden, but I cannot concentrate on the task if I am worrying about you."

"I don't think I can bear to sit there waiting, not knowing what has happened to you."

"Nothing will happen to me. We will deal with Mr. Fellows and then put this all behind us. It will be over in a few hours and we shall spend the rest of the day making up for the years we have missed."

He looked so worried, so tormented, that she felt she had no choice but to agree. "I do not want to hinder you in any way. It would break me if you got hurt because you were looking after me."

Henry Fernall marched into the study. "Let us get this over with."

A hint of cologne drifted through the air; the woody aroma made her nose itch.

"We are not going to meet royalty," Tristan scoffed.

"One should always leave the house looking their best." Henry tugged at the lapels of his clean coat. "One never knows whom they might meet."

After spending a few minutes copying some of Andrew's notes onto a separate piece of paper, they departed for Brook Street.

During the five-minute carriage ride, no one spoke. Henry Fernall used the opportunity to take a quick nap. Mr. Blackwood spent the time nibbling his fingernails. Isabella sat next to Tristan. Beneath the satin folds of her gown, they held hands.

Had Henry Fernall not agreed to accompany him, Isabella would have insisted on going, too. But she did not want to be a distraction, nor did she wish to spend time in Henry's company.

"Promise me you will be careful." Isabella stood in the doorway of the house in Brook Street. She put her hand on Tristan's chest in the hope it would bring some comfort. Her heart thumped wildly against her ribs. The time for complete honesty was upon them. "Now we have been reunited I cannot bear the thought of living without you."

Tristan closed the small gap between them. "You will never be without me." He took her chin between his finger and thumb and stared deeply into her eyes. "I'm in love with you," he said softly. "Indeed, I have never stopped loving you."

She almost choked on the surge of raw emotion bubbling in her throat. "You are the love of my life. You are my life. Hurry back to me."

Tristan smiled though she could see a flicker of apprehension in his eyes. "With any luck, I shall be back in a few hours and then we can put this business behind us and start again."

"Perhaps I should come, too."

With tender strokes, he caressed her cheek. "We have already discussed it a hundred times or more. I completely misread Mr.

Fellows' character. I have no notion what the gentleman is capable of, and so I need to know you are safe."

"I know. It is just that the time passes so slowly when you are waiting. I shall be beside myself with worry."

Regardless of the fact that they were standing in the doorway, he kissed her once on the mouth. "I'll be back soon."

# CHAPTER 22

*T*he carriage rattled along the streets on its way to Green Park. Blackwood held on to the leather roof strap, his trance-like gaze following the dark shadows outside as they raced past the window.

Tristan studied Lord Fernall's grim expression before checking his pocket watch. "Good, we should have time to take our positions before Fellows arrives."

Lord Fernall folded his arms across his chest. "Do you have a plan?"

"Of course. Mr. Blackwood will demand an explanation for your father's murder before he agrees to hand over the notebook. We will hide in the shrubbery until satisfied we have heard enough and then take him into custody."

Tristan had to admit it was a pretty poor plan. But, from experience, he knew success was often down to luck rather than strategy.

Henry Fernall scoffed. "What? You expect Blackwood here to conduct a coherent conversation. The man is a quivering wreck?"

Blackwood tore his gaze away from the window. "I ... I have no choice in the ... the matter."

Tristan dragged his hand down his face and sighed. Bloody hell. What had seemed like a logical solution to their problem now felt like the naive plot of a novice.

"Have a little faith," Tristan replied in a bid to rouse some confidence in his own ability to succeed.

The carriage rumbled to a halt near the north gate. They alighted quickly, the grey blanket of fog proving to be an advantage as they hoped to be in position before Mr. Fellows arrived.

"The tree is just inside the entrance," Blackwood said, pointing to an eerie shadow in the gloom. "They say many a passerby has stumbled upon a body dangling from a bough."

Lord Fernall muttered under his breath. "Do you always speak such gibberish?"

As they approached the tree, Tristan felt the hairs on his nape jump to attention. A frosty chill shivered through him. The muscles in his abdomen grew uncomfortably tight. The natural flow of the earth's rhythm felt disturbed. Many people said dogs could sense the ominous shift in the atmosphere, said that they whined and yelped to alert their owners of the invisible yet menacing presence.

"Whilst it appears to look like any other tree in the park," Tristan began, "I cannot help but feel repelled by it."

Blackwood stared up at the lowest branch. The wood was smooth in places, light in colour where the bark had worn away. "Do you know what they say about the Dead Man's Tree?"

"No," Lord Fernall said with a sigh. "But I am sure you're going to enlighten us with one of your bizarre tales."

"They say the spirits of the dead walk this path," Blackwood whispered. "Their sad souls linger. People have seen strange shadows, figures in shrouds, a man dressed as a cavalier wielding his sword."

Lord Fernall snorted. "And this morning they will see two fools crouching behind the shrubbery."

"Talking of shrubbery," Tristan began as he checked his watch for the umpteenth time, "we should take our places." He gestured to the row of shrubs four feet or so in front of the tree. "We shall hide here. Mr. Blackwood shall stand in front."

Despite a few moans and mumbles, they took their positions.

"We look utterly ridiculous," Lord Fernall complained as he knelt down next to Tristan. "I don't know why I agreed to come."

"It is almost five. We will not have long to wait."

Minutes passed.

Mr. Blackwood paced back and forth.

A low groan breezed past Tristan's ear. He turned to Lord Fernall. "You need to remain quiet."

Lord Fernall glanced back over his shoulder. "That was not me."

They waited.

"Any sign of him?" Tristan whispered, eager to move from behind the large shrub. It was as though a dark and dangerous presence hovered over him, pressing him down into the earth.

"No."

Tristan checked his watch. Fellows was fifteen minutes late.

"I cannot feel my feet," Lord Fernall grumbled. "How much longer must we crouch here like street urchins scouring for scraps?"

"As long as it takes," Tristan said through clenched teeth, trying desperately not to punch the arrogant lord for his indifference to their plight.

Blackwood cleared his throat. "Wait. I think he's coming."

Through a gap made in the foliage, Tristan witnessed Mr. Fellows approach. The hazy black figure appeared to float through the fog, the image growing more prominent as he came closer. At a distance, one could not detect his features.

Indeed, he looked faceless. A nobody. A hulking soulless mass.

Blackwood sucked in a breath, muttered a croaky curse.

Good Lord! Tristan hoped the man could hold his nerve.

As Fellows came closer, he noticed that the gentleman's coat radiated a golden glow. Tristan blinked to focus. His heart flew up to his throat, thumped wildly in his neck until he struggled to breathe. What had looked like one huge distorted figure now proved to be that of two people.

*Isabella.*

Fellows came to a stop a few feet away from Mr. Blackwood. With his left hand, he held Isabella close to his body, aimed the pistol in his right hand at her stomach.

"Ah, Mr. Blackwood. Forgive me if I kept you waiting. I am usually so punctual, but my hackney was forced to make a call in Brook Street to collect the necessary provisions."

The blood roared in Tristan's ears. He blinked rapidly in an attempt to focus. Isabella appeared unharmed. Her lips were drawn thin though it was not fear that flashed in her eyes; he saw anger.

"Do ... do you have my money?" Blackwood stammered.

Fellows grinned. "Do you have my notebook?"

Blackwood held up the brown book. "Let Lady Fernall go and we can make our trade."

Fellows chuckled. "I am afraid that will not be possible. If I am to leave on the next ship to Calcutta, then I must have some assurance you will not intervene. No, Lady Fernall will be coming with me."

Despite Lord Fernall tugging violently on the sleeve of his coat, Tristan could not contain his volatile emotions. "The hell she will." Tristan marched around the overgrown bush to stand at Mr. Blackwood's side.

Fellows tutted. "I did wonder which bush you had chosen to hide behind. Do you take me for a fool, Lord Morford?"

"Only a fool would think he could get away with murder," Tristan countered. It was hard to take the man seriously when his side-whiskers filled his face. "How did you know I was there?"

Fellows shrugged. "I followed Mr. Blackwood to Lady Fernall's carriage. Even through the fog, I recognised her coachman sitting atop his box. As a gentleman, I assumed you would take the lady home before coming to our assignation. You really are rather predictable."

Tristan's mind raced ahead. Fellows did not know Lord Fernall was hiding behind the bush. He said a silent prayer, hoping the lord's reluctance to participate, coupled with his cowardly nature, would cause him to remain hidden.

"I lack your expertise when it comes to criminal activity." Tristan stared at Isabella. She read his silent plea, nodded inconspicuously as a means of reassurance. "As you appear to have the upper hand, perhaps you might enlighten us as to your intentions."

"I want the notebook. I intend to leave here with Lady Fernall. She will remain my companion until I am safely aboard ship. You will not attempt to follow me, but will accept my word that she will be released unharmed."

Tristan snorted. "Why would I trust you when you have lied and deceived me these last few days? You have entered my home under false pretences, merely to pry." Indeed, the man had been left alone for an hour in Tristan's study giving him ample time to rummage through the desk drawers.

"Desperate men do desperate things."

"So you had no real interest in Miss Smythe?" Tristan was determined to keep Mr. Fellows talking. Hearing his confession would ease Tristan's conscience. Whilst all the evidence indicated Fellows was guilty, he could not rely solely on the word of Mr. Blackwood. Nor could he completely trust Andrew's attempt at uncovering a motive.

"Miss Smythe is a delight, but needs must. I am sure Mr. Chandler will be thrilled to have her on his arm."

"What did my mother pay you to attack Miss Smythe in the Holbrooks' garden?"

"She did not pay me." Fellows' eyes flashed with amusement. "When she told me of her plan, I was grateful for the opportunity to distract you. Your mother is a woman riddled with resentment. She would do anything to prevent you from marrying this delightful creature at my side. Who do you think told me Lady Fernall lived in Brook Street?"

Isabella gasped.

Damn it all.

His mother had left him no choice. She could stay in Ripon indefinitely. When he married Isabella, he would not have his mother interfering.

"Does my mother know that you killed Lord Fernall?"

"She sees me as a friend and ally, one who cares about Miss Smythe's happiness. She has no interest in anything beyond that." He gestured to the notebook in Mr. Blackwood's hand. "Now, sunrise is fast approaching. You will give me the notebook and we shall be on our way."

Tristan suppressed his agitation; he had to find a way to stall him.

"Do you know what is written in the notebook?"

Fellows narrowed his gaze. "I'm sure you have read it, so I have nothing to hide. Your brother intimated it contained numerous witness statements proving my illegitimacy."

"You were heard arguing with Lord Fernall over money. You're listed as a participant in the sordid parties he held at Highley Grange. You were seen breaking his neck and carrying him down the stairs."

"All conjecture. You have no proof."

"The notebook is proof," Isabella said quietly.

"There are statements from peers, from the servants who

tended your mother." He gestured to Mr. Blackwood. "We can all attest to your guilt."

Fellows glanced down at the pistol in his hand. "I think you forget that I hold the winning card in this game. If I am to hang for one murder, then I may as well hang for two."

Tristan's steely reserve wavered, but he held firm. "I suppose a man capable of murdering his own father is capable of anything," he said, though the thought of doing away with his mother had some appeal.

"He was not my father," Mr. Fellows snapped, suddenly appearing more than a little disgruntled. "My father was a decent, honest man, kind and considerate. He was not a debauched heathen who would sell his soul if he thought it would enhance his pleasure."

"Pleasure was what my husband lived for," Isabella said. "There were times when he drove me to despair, times when I thought to kill him myself."

Fellows snorted. "I wish you had. It would have saved me the trouble."

The comment was perhaps as close to a confession as they would get. It would be enough to convince Lord Fernall to make a statement.

"I know he had a way of belittling those around him," Isabella said with an air of melancholy. "He had a way of making others feel worthless."

"When I refused to participate in his dissipated games, he said I was too weak, spineless, that he was ashamed I was his son."

"I understand." She spoke softly; her tone held a musical quality like a soothing melody drifting on a breeze. "He once told me he was ashamed that I was his wife. When I questioned his own morals and values, he told me he would tell all those he knew how inadequate I had proved to be, that I was a failure."

Tristan's heart ached for her. Although he knew she spoke in order to extract information from Mr. Fellows, he could sense the truth in her words.

"He was a spiteful, selfish prig. When I discovered the true character of the man, I begged him to keep the nature of our relationship a secret," Fellows grumbled. "But he taunted me, threatened to tell all those he knew that I had a penchant for debauchery. He put his arm around me and said ..." Fellows broke off on a curse.

"What did he say?" Isabella asked.

"He said that wickedness is in the blood."

Well, Samuel Fernall had been right about that.

"Then you must prove him wrong, Mr. Fellows," Isabella said with an air of determination.

"It is too late. I've no choice but to return to India." Fellows pushed Isabella forward, jabbed the barrel of the pistol into her side. "Give the notebook to Lady Fernall."

"What about my money?" Blackwood asked.

"You'll get nothing from me. If I'm to move abroad, I must be frugal. Hand over the book."

Tristan doubted Fellows would pull the trigger, but he would not take the chance.

"Give him the notebook, Mr. Blackwood."

Blackwood grumbled and mumbled at his side. With trembling fingers, he held the book out in front of him.

A pained groan and a sudden shuffling from behind the bush captured their attention.

Lord Fernall shot up, punching wildly at the air.

Tristan muttered a curse.

"Forgive me," Fernall said, his face twisted into a grimace. "Someone prodded me in the back with something sharp." He gestured to a point over his shoulder. "The blighter pinched me on the arm."

Someone? There was not a soul in the park.

Fellows stared at him for the longest time, his eyes growing wide, fearful. Lord Fernall was not a particularly handsome man but his countenance hardly proved terrifying.

"What is that?" Fellows cried, continually blinking as though attempting to clear his vision after waking from slumber.

Lord Fernall appeared most affronted. "Are you referring to me?" He stomped around the bush as though ready to unleash a torrent of abuse and came to stand at Tristan's side.

It was then they noticed that Mr. Fellows was not looking at anyone in particular. One minute he was squinting, the next his eyes were wide again.

"What do you want with me?" Fellows thrust Isabella forward, using her body as a shield.

"We want you to let Lady Fernall go," Tristan replied, though he had some doubt as to whether the gentleman was speaking to him. With Mr. Fellows somewhat distracted, Tristan waited for the right moment to wrestle him to the ground. He turned to Lord Fernall. "The man appears to have lost his mind."

Lord Fernall frowned. "What is he staring at?"

With a sudden gasp, Fellows pushed Isabella to one side and pointed the pistol at the Dead Man's Tree. His hand shook so violently he was liable to shoot any one of them.

As he waved the pistol back and forth, they all ducked and scrambled out of the line of fire.

Isabella rushed to stand at Tristan's side. He clutched her hand briefly, resisted the urge to pull her into his arms and apologise for his terrible miscalculation. "Find some way to distract him," he whispered.

She replied with a confident nod. "What is that over there? I see it … a tall, black shadow … it is coming towards us."

Mr. Fellows' frantic gaze flitted left and right.

Tristan took the opportunity to charge at him. He grabbed Fellows around the waist and took him down to the ground.

A loud crack echoed through the air.

Isabella screamed.

Tristan waited for the pain, for the draining feeling that accompanied a heavy loss of blood. He patted his chest, checked his palm fearing the skin would be stained red.

In a state of panic, Mr. Fellows scrambled to his feet. With one more glance at the tree, he raced towards the gate and disappeared into the mist.

"The ball hit the tree," Blackwood said, helping Tristan to his feet. "Quick. Mr. Fellows is getting away."

Sucking in a ragged breath, Tristan took Isabella's hand and made for the gate with Blackwood and Lord Fernall in tow.

"I shall be glad to be away from this place," Lord Fernall panted as he glanced at the tree. "I am telling you there was someone behind me whilst I was hiding back there."

Unable to suppress a smirk, Tristan said, "What do you mean? Are you saying that a ghost attacked you?"

Fernall grunted as they passed through the gate. "You may mock—"

The horses' high-pitched squeals and a coachman's gruff, masculine curse overpowered the sound of the peddlers' carts rattling along the street. Numerous shrieks and cries were interspersed with what Tristan suspected was the crunch of breaking bones.

The sight of Mr. Fellows' crumpled body sprawled across the road stopped them dead in their tracks.

# CHAPTER 23

*T*ristan pulled Isabella closer. "Don't look. It is not a pretty sight."

She buried her head in his chest. "Oh, it is so terrible."

"He got trampled by the horses and crushed by the carriage wheels," someone shouted from the small crowd that had stopped to observe the horrific scene. "His neck's broken."

Tristan sighed. The irony was not lost on him.

The coachman rushed over to examine the body. "The man came out of nowhere. I never even got a chance to tug on the reins," he said as the crowd offered words of reassurance upon witnessing his distress.

"I doubt there is any point calling a doctor," Lord Fernall said. "But we need to be sure he is dead."

Tristan glanced at the body. Blood trickled from a wound on his head. Fellows' eyes were open, wide, empty. Had there been even the smallest sign of life, it would have been accompanied by painful cries and groans. "He is dead. Of that I am certain."

"What do we do now?" Isabella straightened but turned her back to the disturbing sight.

"I shall handle this," Lord Fernall said in his usual authoritative tone. "Leave now. Mr. Blackwood will assist me."

Suspicion flared. For a man who had shown nothing but disinterest from the moment they had knocked his door, Lord Fernall must have had an epiphany. Either that or he imagined Mrs. Forester would lavish him with attention when he described stumbling upon the distressing event.

"What will you say?" Tristan asked. It occurred to him that, whether Lord Fernall accepted the fact or not, Mr. Fellows was his brother and by rights, it was his responsibility to deal with the situation.

"My father saw fit to degrade the Fernall name. I will not add to my burden by revealing he was murdered by his illegitimate son." Fernall cleared his throat. "Whilst I would like to wipe my hands of the whole affair, I see an opportunity to deal with things in a quiet, unassuming manner."

"There are a number of witnesses who will say he simply ran out into the road." Tristan glanced at the group whispering to each other and pointing at the body. "It was an accident. With such dense fog, no one will be surprised."

"We will just be two more passing witnesses," Lord Fernall replied. "That is if Blackwood here can hold his nerve."

Tristan observed Mr. Blackwood whose countenance expressed nothing but relief.

"What happened to Mr. Fellows' pistol?" Tristan asked. "There's every chance someone heard the loud crack."

"I have it." Mr. Blackwood quickly opened the front of his coat to reveal the metal object tucked into the band of his breeches.

"Close your damn coat, man, before someone notices," Lord Fernall whispered through gritted teeth.

"You will have to say you heard what sounded like a shot," Tristan said. "Suggest someone may have attempted to rob him in the park and that was why he was running."

"We shall remain here and offer a statement." Lord Fernall

nodded. "But before you go, I would like your permission to burn the notebook. I trust that the information gleaned will be kept in confidence."

Tristan had no desire to read of Samuel Fernall's debauched lifestyle, nor did he wish to be in possession of an item that linked him to Mr. Fellows. Besides, the sooner they put the past behind them, the better.

"Under the circumstances," he said, glancing once more at the crumpled body, "I doubt we shall have need of it. You may keep it providing Lady Fernall is in agreement."

Isabella nodded. "It is of no use to me." She tugged his arm and whispered, "What about the sketch?"

"Don't worry." Offering a sly smirk, Tristan tapped the breast pocket of his coat. "It is safe." He turned his attention to Lord Fernall. "I shall call on you tomorrow to see how you fared."

Lord Fernall inclined his head. "If I am not at home, you may find me at White's."

They had taken but a few steps when Lord Fernall called out to Isabella. "If you still wish to remain at Highley Grange, then you have my word you will be left to live there in peace."

She pursed her lips, remained silent for a moment. "Thank you, but I shall make my own arrangements. After all that has happened, I cannot envisage living there again."

Lord Fernall made no protest. Indeed, a faint smile touched the corners of his mouth. "As you wish. You may forward any extra expenses you incur as a consequence to my man in Jermyn Street."

Tristan clenched his jaw. It took all the effort he possessed not to curse the pompous lord and inform him Isabella would not need his charity again.

"Thank you," she said politely. "But my current situation is adequate for my needs."

As they walked away, Tristan decided it was time to address

her current situation, to make her an offer he hoped she would not refuse.

As previously agreed, Dawes was waiting on the corner of Bolton Street. Tristan helped Isabella into the carriage, conveyed instructions to the coachman before climbing into the conveyance.

Tristan cleared his throat. "If I ever ask you to remain at home again, you have permission to curse me to the devil." Guilt still ate away at him when he thought of Isabella greeting a murderer at the door.

"I think I would rather be abducted by Mr. Fellows than be forced to squat behind a bush with Henry Fernall."

He suspected her amusing comment was said purely to ease his conscience.

"Do you think it wise to call on Henry tomorrow?" Isabella continued. "Judging by the stern look on your face I thought you were about to strangle him with his cravat."

"Trust me. I was tempted." Indeed, it had taken a tremendous amount of willpower not to punch Henry Fernall hard in his gut. "I don't know how he can look you in the eye when he behaved so appallingly."

Isabella smiled. "I know, but I cannot be angry with him. Had it not been for the hauntings at Highley Grange I would not have approached you to ask for your help. And then we might never have discovered the truth."

His chest felt hollow when he considered the possibility that he could have lived his life never knowing about the cruel deception that had forced them apart. He would have gone to his grave always believing she did not love him.

"When you put it like that, I feel an immense gratitude for his cruel and overbearing manner." He stared at her for a moment, at the soft full lips he longed to taste, at the dark brown eyes that had the ability to see into his soul. "What will you do now?"

Her curious gaze drifted over his face. "Well, between us I imagine we will have a busy few days. Besides your appointment with Henry, you promised to call on Mr. Chandler. And no doubt Miss Smythe will need someone unbiased to talk to, a lady who will give her an honest opinion."

"True. And I have yet to inform my mother she will be leaving for Ripon today."

"Then you promised to take me on a shopping expedition. You promised to buy me something bold and bright as you know how much I like yellow." She folded her arms across her chest. "So, I'm afraid you will have to put up with me for a little while longer."

He couldn't help but smile. Why could she not just say she wanted to spend more time with him?

He rubbed his chin. "If you're in need of something to do, perhaps you might help me redecorate some of the rooms in Bedford Square. I find I have been wallowing in the darkness for far too long and need some vibrancy in my life."

She raised a brow. "Most gentlemen prefer subdued colours. I doubt you will want to sit at home staring at yellow walls all day long."

He shrugged. "I won't need to. We will only redesign the rooms for your personal use." An image of her wearing a sheer, diaphanous nightgown as she lounged on a bright pink chaise flashed into his mind.

"My personal use?"

"Well, I would want you to feel at home. Of course, we will share a bedchamber. There will be no sleeping in separate rooms." Just thinking about waking up next to her each morning caused his heart to race. "And we will spend part of the year at Kempston Hall."

He expected to see a brilliant smile light up her face, but her expression grew solemn. "Forgive me for being obtuse," she said quietly, "but what exactly are you suggesting?"

Did he need to spell it out? Were his intentions not perfectly clear?

Then again, he suspected her experiences had made her cautious.

He crossed the carriage to sit at her side, pushed the stray curl from her face. "I love you. I have loved you from the moment I met you and will love you until I draw my last breath. Marry me, Isabella. Take your place at my side as it was always destined to be."

She swallowed deeply as she stared into his eyes. "Tristan, I love you more than anything. What you offer sounds like heaven here on earth, but what if I am barren and cannot give you a child? A gentleman in your position must produce an heir. The few times with Samuel—"

He put his fingers on her lips. "Do you honestly think I care about that?" Even now her thoughts were only for him. Why had he doubted her all those years ago? "My cousin Harold can have what's left should that prove to be the case."

She placed her hand on his cheek, kissed him tenderly on the mouth. "You are the love of my life. I want to spend my days laughing with you, my nights indulging in far more illicit pleasures."

His heart swelled, as did another part of his anatomy. "We could elope." He never wanted to be without her again. "We could ride in this carriage all the way to Scotland. Pretend the last five years never existed."

She gazed longingly into his eyes. "It sounds wonderful. But we cannot abandon Mr. Chandler and Miss Smythe. Had they not agreed to marry, things could have ended so differently for us. And I have a feeling they are going to need our help."

She was right, of course.

He gave a weary sigh. "I doubt five years of daily prayer and a vow of chastity would reform Matthew Chandler."

The corners of her mouth twitched in amusement. "Is that how you spent your five years in the monastery?"

"I prayed every night." *Begged* was perhaps the appropriate word. "I prayed that the Lord would ease my pain and torment."

"Well, you can take comfort in the fact that he listened." She placed her hand on his leg, caressed his thigh with sensual strokes. "Do you recall how excited we were the day we eloped? Do you recall how our excitement led to a rather amorous interlude in the carriage?"

"I have never forgotten it. Indeed, I have revisited the memory many times over the years."

"Well, we may not have the opportunity to elope, but we could certainly take a ride to Kempston. I should like to see the gardens again, to frolic next to the fountain."

He rather liked the train of her thoughts. "And on the way, we could find a way to sate our excitement."

"I am sure there will be time to find more than one way to accomplish our task."

Without needing to hear another word, he shot out of his seat, opened the window and relayed their instructions to the coachman. Closing the window and the blind, he dropped back into the seat next to her.

"Kempston it is then." He took hold of her chin and kissed her with five years of lust, love and longing. "Promise me we shall marry upon our return."

She pulled down the blind on her window, gathered her gown and sat astride him. "I promise to marry you upon our return. Bloodthirsty hounds and wailing ghosts could not keep us apart. I promise to love you all of my life."

The End

**What You Promised**

**Book 4 in the Anything for Love Series**

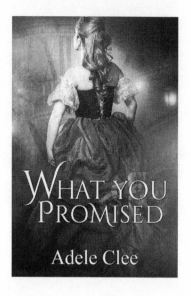

He promised his name and his protection.

But not his love.

Made in the USA
Columbia, SC
02 April 2023

14679367R00140